THE LIFE AND TRIALS OF BENJAMIN TATE

ALAN FELDBERG

Print ISBN: 978-1-916978-90-4

For Leeza, without whom Benjamin Tate would have lived and died in a long-forgotten short story.

PROLOGUE

There is a boy on a bench. The bench is beside a park and there is a skittish breeze blowing. It is poking about at the dropped and fallen things; litter and dry leaves. There is a girl sitting beside the boy. He is talking to her but he doesn't believe what he is saying. He is only saying it because he thinks he should. But he doesn't believe what he is saying and is starting to waver. She would only have to look at him. But she does not look at him. She looks at her phone and begins deleting all his pictures. It is 3.37pm.

A mile away there is a mother with a pushchair walking along the pavement. She is wearing stockings and a short skirt. An hour ago she was outside a door. She had rested her forehead and knuckles against it and couldn't decide whether to go in or not. The child in the pushchair is wriggling. Something sharp is jabbing in her back and she keeps shifting in her seat. It is making it difficult for her mother to walk in a straight line, and she thinks vaguely of shopping trolleys.

Between her and the park there is a roundabout. Three roads lead into it. It used to be a quiet part of town with very few cars, but the town has grown quickly in recent years and the roundabout is always busy now. Local residents have argued for a pedestrian crossing, but there isn't one yet.

The boy is still talking to the girl, but she decides now that she has heard enough and stands up and walks away. The boy watches her. How she fills her jeans. Even now he can't help looking. *I'm doing the right thing*, he thinks, *this is the right decision*. He watches her until she crests a grassy slope and then vanishes behind it and then he watches the empty space where she was. He is a runner. He could catch up to her very easily if he wanted. But he stands up and walks to the car park. He will think back to this moment many times. He will think if he'd acted differently none of the bad things that are about to happen would have happened. It is 3.52pm.

The mother with the pushchair is two hundred yards from the roundabout. She is walking very slowly. She is still thinking about that door and the decision she made. She doesn't know if she is happy or not. She doesn't know if she is good or not. She thinks by now she should know fundamental things like this. 'Sit still,' she says to the top of her daughter's head. Her daughter has blonde hair. It coils at the end like a ribbon drawn over a blade. Neither she nor her husband are blonde and she wonders if her hair will darken as she gets older. 3.58pm.

The boy is in his car now. He is driving along the road that leads to the roundabout. The park is on his right. There is a line of tall trees between the road and the park and the sun is low behind them, casting shadows like corpses across the asphalt. It's his mother's fault. She made him do this. He decides suddenly that he hates his mother and finds comfort in having somewhere to direct his anger. 'I hate you,' he shouts at the windscreen. He bangs the steering wheel and the car veers across the lines. A yellow car coming towards him takes evasive action. 'I hate you,' he shouts again. His anger is turning to rage and the rage is pressing down on his foot. 4.03pm.

The mother's phone vibrates in her pocket and she takes it out to read the message. 'It hurts, Mummy,' the child says. It is the corner of a milk carton sticking out the top of a shopping bag in the hold beneath her. But the child doesn't know that. She knows only that something is hurting her and she can't get away from it. She shifts again and the rubber wheels of the pushchair splay outwards and it jars to a halt. Her mother is still looking at her phone and bumps into the back of it. 'Ruby! Can you just sit still!' She puts her phone away and immediately feels it vibrate again. She tries to ignore it but knowing there is another message makes her anxious. She begins to walk quicker. She is one hundred yards from the roundabout.

There is a bus stop just before the roundabout. The bus is late today and there are more people waiting than usual. They will be the nearest witnesses. Some will remain frozen to the spot, others will rush instinctively towards where the noise came from.

The boy's car is off-white. He knows he is driving too fast but he is nineteen and he is upset. He is thinking of the girl and their last time. He is approaching the roundabout now. He can see it just in front of him. There are no cars there for once so he will just glide into it and let the curve slingshot him round.

The mother is also at the roundabout. Her phone keeps vibrating and the child is still squirming. She feels like she might scream. She closes her eyes but keeps walking. She feels the pushchair jolt and lurch as a wheel tips into the gutter. The child falls to the right and would have toppled out were she not strapped in.

The boy is still thinking about their last time when the kerb breaks free from the pavement and rushes at him. It moves much faster than he expects. He brakes hard and yanks at the steering wheel but his two-tonne car is an unstoppable force and won't stop. A shape appears in front of him, an object seemingly conjured out of thin air. It flashes on the windscreen and then his momentum carries him right through it. The mother gasps. She pulls back on the handles, but the handles are no longer there. 4.07pm.

The people at the bus stop hear the sound. It is violent and sudden. It rips up the street and makes heads turn towards it. One of the men at the bus stop drops into a crouch. He is a veteran and loud bangs always startle him.

The car is not moving now. The only thing moving is a tiny plastic boot hanging from the rear-view mirror. It is swinging excitedly, toe-poking the cracked windscreen. *Tap, tap, tap* it goes against the glass. The boy – his name is Benjamin Tate – is sitting in his car and looking at the buckled bonnet in front of him. He doesn't feel any pain. He takes the car out of gear and lifts the handbrake, and then reaches up and stills the plastic boot.

The mother with the pushchair no longer has the pushchair. She is sitting down on the pavement. Or has been thrown down. About five yards away there is a mess of fabric and plastic and steel. From somewhere within it a thin white liquid is seeping over the road in jagged streams. That is the milk. The mother begins crawling towards it. 4.08pm.

Nearby someone is crying. It is a child. Her eyes have been covered by an adult's hands but she is still crying. The man at the bus stop who had crouched down is now running towards the roundabout. He is not looking at the steaming car, but the broken things left in its wake. He is unsure what he will do when he gets there.

Benjamin Tate gets out of his car and then falls immediately to the ground. His right kneecap has been split in two by the back of the ignition key and a bone in his lower leg has broken through the skin. It looks like the bottom of an upturned tree. He notices this objectively but still feels no pain and begins climbing to his feet again.

The girl who had been sitting on the bench is called Madeline. She has reached where she is going now. She doesn't call it home. She opens the front door quietly and tiptoes up the stairs. She wants to slip into her room unnoticed and pull the covers up over her head. And that's all she wants.

Not far away a woman is sitting at her kitchen table waiting for her son to return. She would like to talk to him about things but it has been difficult lately. She has written him a letter instead and placed it on his pillow. She is waiting for him to get home and read it.

It is remarkable how quickly a crowd gathers. In the coming days people who weren't there will say they were and the stories told will all be different. It will be a conversation piece and then it will be nothing at all. There are paramedics at the scene now. They are moving about in their dark-green uniforms quickly but without panic. One of them places a tentative hand on the mother's shoulder but the mother, crouched over and holding a bundle of something in her arms, doesn't notice. Two police officers are talking to bystanders and two more are laying down cones. The sun is still shining. It glistens on the back of a tinfoil blanket and a magpie twitches its black-mirror eyes.

Benjamin Tate is no longer beside his white car. He has been lifted onto a stretcher and a face is leaning over and looking down at him. He watches the mouth move and notices randomly that the tongue is pierced. His eyes close and almost immediately he becomes aware that the pain has started now. It is astonishing pain, it is almost beyond pain and it blocks everything else out. Without warning he is sick all over himself but not all the sick leaves his mouth and he splutters and chokes. When he opens his eyes again he is in an ambulance and there is a needle in his arm. The pierced tongue is still there, clicking against teeth. He begins to feel a black creeping thing move through his body. The pain starts to fade and when he realises this he experiences relief like he's never known. His mother is there too. Where has she come from? He doesn't care. He doesn't hate her really. He vomits again. Everything will be all right. She will take him away from... from what? He has a vague sense of something awful having happened but it's beyond his grasp. The black creeping thing is moving all through him now. He feels his mother's hand on his brow. She is young, hardly older than he is, and that doesn't seem strange to him. She is rocking him. He is so light. The curtains of his room flutter in the night breeze. A lamp glows weakly in the corner. It is late. She looks tired, his mother. He is tired also. He will sleep. The black creeping thing fills him up. 4.46pm.

The mother with the pushchair is also in an ambulance. She is sitting motionless, staring at the opposite wall with a blanket over her shoulders. A woman who is trained in these things is talking to her quietly. Outside, a cloud bank is forming on the horizon. The sun drops behind it and the air around the roundabout cools. Goosebumps on arms. A hush descends. On the road a blanket is placed over something before it is scooped up and carried away. Whatever is left behind, whatever essence remains there on the stained ground, is taken by the wind.

Between 5pm and 6pm 13,026 phone calls are made by residents of the town. Of these, 13,024 are insignificant. But the other two are not insignificant and the people who receive them are forever changed.

The woman who was sitting at the kitchen table – she is Benjamin Tate's mother – is still there. The last of the day is fading but she has not got up to turn the light on. Nothing moves. When the phone rings it startles the room. She listens for a few minutes and afterwards she remains at the table a little longer, as still as she had been before. She stands up abruptly. She goes to search for her husband. When she finds him she talks in one long rush. Their life as they knew it is over. 5.13pm.

On the outskirts of the town another man is driving home. His mind has shut down. He couldn't understand what his wife was saying at first. 'Calm down,' he said, 'speak slower.' But eventually he was made to understand and his mind shut down. His colleagues should not have let him drive. They realise this now. In the coming months their awkwardness around him will become unbearable. He will learn that grief sits on your face like a disfigurement and people don't want to look at it.

10.56pm. The storm that has been threatening has finally arrived. It soaks the pavements and floods the park. The roundabout is deserted now. The emergency vehicles have gone. The crowds and the cones have gone. Rain glistens in the glare of streetlights shining down into empty spaces. But in the morning the traffic will return. The people will be back. And all will be as it was.

PART 1

CHAPTER ONE

At first he ran because the older boys chased him, then he ran because he liked it, then he ran because he was the best. He rose while the house still slept and put his trainers on; pale early morning light through the window, a low, heavy sky over wet grass. He breathed deeply as he walked down the path, filling his lungs with new air. The letter was still on the windowsill in his room. It had arrived three days earlier and he'd opened it not knowing what he wanted it to say. Either way it would be bad news. Big things have a way of smashing up little things. His future was a big thing. His current whims were little things. He shook the night's stiffness out of his legs and then began, a few short strides to ease into it, stepping over snails inching hazardously across the pavement. The street was empty. The only sound was his light step. He thought about the letter. It was only fourteen lines long. What would she say? She hadn't seen it yet. Like him, she'd been waiting for it.

The world was his own at that time of the morning. He passed the closed curtains, the parked cars, the handmade banner on the door saying, '*Welcome home, Daddy*', each letter a different colour. In the silent gardens spider webs wet with dew hung like fine lace between branches and over low bushes. He moved onto the hump in the middle of the road. His arms swung loose at his sides. *Tap-tap, tap-tap.* He turned into the park. How many times had he done this, how many laps? By now he knew each swell, each dip where ice would gather on winter nights. He passed under the arch of oak trees. He passed the croquet lawn and the cracked cement of what had once been a tennis court. He passed the playground where he met her.

'I know you,' she had said to him then. It was two years ago. She was sitting on a swing, rocking gently back and forth below trees full of summer. The toes of her boots bounced over the ground as they dragged.

'Do you?' he asked.

'Well, I don't know you. But I've seen you before.'

'I've seen you, too.' They had actually gone to the same school, though he doubted she'd have noticed him. She was one of those girls who boys like him stared at from afar, who entertained wicked thoughts about and blushed wildly at even a hint of contact, no matter how meaningless or impersonal. He was terrified of her really, of all girls, but her especially. He recalled the litany of stories that circulated through the corridors, the things they said she did at the sorts of parties boys like him only heard about afterwards. He didn't believe all of them, was even too innocent still to understand all of them. What did those words mean? What acts, specifically, did they signify? She was dressed now all in black; black jeans and a heavy black jumper that drowned her slight frame. He thought how out of place she looked, amidst the climbing frame and the slide and the seesaws.

'Don't you get bored?' she asked him. He glanced at her

quickly, nonplussed. She looked over his shoulder to the fields behind him. 'I've seen you. Just running round and round?'

'Oh. I guess I do. Sometimes.'

'Why don't you stop then? And don't just stand there, you're making me uncomfortable. Sit.'

'I'm going to America on an athletics scholarship. I'm good enough. I'm not going yet, I'm still too young, but when I'm older I'm going.'

Had he really told her then, before he even knew her name? Surely, he wasn't so bold or so boastful. The American Dream, that's what his mother had called it once, lamely, he thought, but that's what he now called it as well. It was something private, a treasure he kept hidden in his pocket. He took it out sometimes, when no one was around, to examine it, to hold it up to the light and roll in between thumb and forefinger until it reflected his best face back at him. It never failed to excite him, to restore him somehow. It was his secret superpower.

He heard his voice telling her how often he ran, and how far and how fast. He told her about some of the races he'd already won and would still win.

'It's not easy to get one, a place I mean, but I will.'

Suddenly he faltered. The sun was glaring at him from up high. It made him sweat. Wasn't she hot? Maybe it wasn't the sun making him sweat. He remembered her lips, how they pursed around the cigarette, how her cheeks hollowed as she sucked hard. He remembered the smoke filling the cave of her mouth before the wind reached in and scooped it away.

'I actually believe you,' she said. He was still looking at her mouth.

He turned past the car park and floated down the gentle slope that led over the path he'd arrived on. The footprints of his first lap were pressed into the grass in front of him, running away into the distance like the tracks of a faster rival. He remembered his first race. The thrill of flowing around the bend, slipping round shoulder after shoulder. The ease of it: the school, then the club, then the county – they hadn't found anyone who could beat him. He looped again around the croquet lawn, the tennis court. He was gaining speed. His stride was lengthening, his lungs were opening. He was running fast. He could always tell. It felt like it was someone else then. The cool air rushed over his hot skin. He passed the playground where he met her.

'Come,' she'd said to him late one night, closing the door silently behind them. It was their first night, or his first night, at least. 'But be quiet.' He remembered standing motionless on the rug for what seemed like ages, peering out blindly until black shapes and objects began to emerge blacker than the blackness behind them. He followed her as she picked her way between them. His heart was drumming heavily beneath his ribcage. He could make out a table, a bookcase, the large, lighter rectangle of the French doors behind their blinds. The click of his step softened as he crossed a carpet. 'Be careful here,' she whispered, before descending a wooden staircase that creaked beneath her weight. He followed cautiously, hands tracing the walls, feeling the lip of each stair with the soles of his shoes. Suddenly a light was switched on and he found himself standing in a sparse basement. There was a dartboard and a chalk line scratched on the cement floor, a threadbare couch, a picture of an old sailing ship behind a glass frame. The artist had painted it small, a tiny, vulnerable thing ill-equipped to cross the vast ocean in front of it. He sympathised.

She walked past him and opened a small fridge humming to itself against the wall. She took out a bottle of water and gulped thirstily before holding it out towards him. He shook his head and she had another mouthful before putting it back. He wondered how such a small frame could absorb so much. She seemed unaffected, undiminished. He didn't know how he'd got there. In one swift movement, she pulled her vest over her head.

She. She is Madeline. She is red fingernails and tight vests. She is purple hair matching purple boots. She is loud music and strange parties and sweat in dark corners of dark rooms. When she was sixteen she and some friends had a competition to see how many boys they could sleep with in a single summer. Madeline's number was twenty-three. Or that was the number she told them. It was half the real number, but it was more than enough. Of course, she knew what people thought. She thought it herself. And it was all true. Yet here she was again. He was a little timid for her liking, a little young in manner. He stood there gazing at the canvas like he'd never seen a painting before. But she'd always liked the name Ben. Had she had a Ben before? She couldn't recall. She hadn't always known names. She took a step towards him.

Sweat soaked his T-shirt and rolled down his face but his legs felt good. He looked down and saw his knees pumping like pistons, propelling his body forward. Leaves zipped beneath him and disappeared forever. The machine powered on. He ran when he was confused, he ran when he was worried, when he was annoyed, elated, melancholy. He ran to escape things and to find things. He saw a second runner emerge from the path in front of him, an intruder, a hunched slogger labouring up the slope with neither grace nor love. He was about one hundred yards ahead. He passed the playground where he met her.

'Was it your first time?' she asked him afterwards. They were lying on the couch. He was limp and exposed and acutely aware of his nakedness. A slideshow of impossible images, each harder to believe than the last, played in his head.

'No. Course not.' But he knew it was obvious. He'd seen films, and read things.

'Ah, that's sweet.'

'Was it yours?' He scrunched his eyes together. *Stupid, stupid, stupid.*

He remembered the graffiti scribbled on the side of the climbing frame – '*Maddi sucks cock for rock*'. He'd read it countless times. Maddi didn't have to mean Madeline. What else then? Maddison? He didn't know any Maddisons. Her small body rose and fell as she breathed beside him. Her thigh stuck to his. Her arm hung over his chest. The refrigerator still hummed quietly in the corner. He looked down at himself and thought how absurd he was.

The middle-aged slogger was less than twenty yards in front. His head was rocking and his feet landed on the ground like weights. He glanced behind and seemed to slump further into his shoulders. Ten yards. Eight. Five. Two... But Ben didn't rush straight past. Instead, he slowed his pace and settled on the slogger's shoulder. The slogger glanced back again and waved his arm, spluttering something that snatched on his breath. But still Ben didn't pass. He trotted lightly just behind and watched the heavy body struggle. He looked at the short, shuffling stride. He saw how the white knees buckled inwards under the weight and how the feet scraped over the top of the grass. Ben often did this in races. Sometimes he broke early and had the track to himself, but often he left it late, until the last possible moment, just watching and waiting until there was hope to snatch away.

They passed the playground where he met her. '*Maddi sucks cock for rock.*' He could surge clear at any moment. Just one subtle shift would take him away. It would be effortless. But still he waited. Gradually the slogger's pace slowed. Ben drew level and he could see the mouth hanging open, the red, overheating face, the little belly below his T-shirt, that middle-age spread. And yet. And yet here he still was. In spite of all that. Fighting the tide. Dragging behind him the weight of all the hours and days and years spent behind a desk, in a car, on the couch. Ben saw the hair thinning on top, greying at the side. He saw the tension in the shoulders, the joints grinding in their sockets and the aging, flaking muscles struggling to match the spirit.

He began to slow, letting the slogger pull away again. Two yards. Five yards. Eight. Ten. He saw the slogger look around as he passed the croquet lawn. Twenty yards. Ben let the gap open further. He passed the playground where he met her. He was hardly moving. Fifty yards. He stopped and walked for a few paces and then sat down on the grass. Steam rose off his skin. He didn't know he wouldn't run again for more than twenty years.

CHAPTER TWO

Tim woke up at 4.07am. Not by choice. He remained motionless on the mattress, listening to her snore softly beside him. When he could stand it no longer he got up. He was deliberately clamorous. He muttered. He sighed heavily. He bumped the bed with his knee. At the door he stopped and turned around. She hadn't stirred. 'Urgh,' he said resentfully. *Sleep*, he thought, *is like sex and money; it only matters when you don't have it.*

Downstairs, he stood in the centre of the living room, still a little dazed, trying to decide what to do next. It was dark. All around him the house carried on with its clandestine doings; electronic devices set and reset, creaks creaked in far corners, pipes clunked hollowly behind walls and beneath floorboards. The drawer of the cabinet was still on its side on the floor. He looked at it ruefully, absently running a finger along a cut on his hand. Yesterday he'd tried to open one of its drawers. It had snagged on its rollers and all at once something inside him, something that wasn't him but had recently inhabited him, something ominous that he was wary of, had erupted forth. It had shaken the drawer with unconstrained rage until it broke away and then it had lifted the drawer high and slammed it into the floor. The panels had shattered and bounced and a jagged splinter had ripped his skin.

'Daddy?' Ruby had been standing there. 'Why are you shouting?'

He yawned deeply and walked to the back door and opened it. A blast of cold air hit him. He closed his eyes and let his head rest against the frame. It had started happening more frequently, these early mornings. He'd turned the clock around, he'd tried herbal teas, mindfulness, even acupuncture, but whatever it was that crept out of its hole to unsettle him in the dead of night still came. He knew what waking early meant, or could mean. He didn't feel depressed though. Tired, yes, all the time. But who wouldn't be if they kept waking up at this ungodly hour? And what did depression feel like anyway? He was of a generation that grew up thinking some people were happier than others, some better behaved, some more confident. He was mistrustful of labels that explained away personalities.

'You should see someone,' Beth said to him.

'I'm just not sleeping well, that's all.'

'You seem to be doing okay when Ruby cries at night.'

In the garden the grass was long and wet. It soaked his toes as he walked. Petrichor. That was the word for this smell. It had something to do with rainfall and sediment. How did he know that? In three hours he would leave for work. It would be another eighteen hours before he could go back to bed. The prospect filled him with such desperation that he tried to cry it out but just coughed once, a sort of choked splutter, and then fell silent. A soft purple was creeping up the horizon. There was birdsong. Away over the rooftops a church bell rang. Someone would be up there now, at the top of that ancient spire, heaving away at the rope.

He considered going for a run. He leant down towards his

toes, got only as far as his knees and then stood up again. He hated running. He should've started earlier or not at all. Now it was all just gear crunching. His joints had set and weren't inclined to unset. He remembered that young buck who had been running in the park the last time, prancing on his shoulder, mocking him with his youth and fitness. He looked down at his belly, it was still there, the stubborn, antagonising little shit. Not so little. He tried again to touch his toes, hung in limbo for a few moments with his arms dangling. He imagined how the pavement would jar his legs and make his hips ache. No, there would be no runs today. He stood up again.

Ruby, wrapped in her duvet, was standing on the grass behind him.

'Oh,' he said. 'Hello. What are you doing up?' He couldn't see her face clearly in the gloom. 'Couldn't sleep? Nor me. I guess my brain is too full up with things.'

She contemplated this, then said, 'Everything disappears from my head when I'm asleep. Then new stuff comes in when I wake up. But if I do wake up and it's still dark I don't use my normal eyes. I use my sleepy eyes to look around the room. Then I can go straight back to sleep.'

'Your sleepy eyes?'

'These.' She jutted her face forward and scrunched her eyes into slits. He collected her up in his arms and carried her to the porch and sat down. She was so small still, so impossibly small. No one believed she was three until she started talking.

'What do you think,' he asked her, 'about having a baby brother or sister?'

'Would you still love me as much?' she asked. She stared at him in that frank, unabashed way that children do.

'Nothing will ever change how much I love you. Or how much your mother loves you. I know she gets grumpy. But we all get grumpy sometimes. Grown-ups can be very silly.' He pondered that word, imagined using it to describe her to her face. He could imagine the response. Beth was so unforgiving these days. She sounded always so put upon. What had he expected of her, when Ruby was born? He hadn't expected her to be so altered. Naively, he thought that becoming a mother would simply add to what was already there.

He looked down. Ruby was fast asleep in his lap, a soft little heap tucked up inside the blanket. Her mouth was open and she was making a low purring sound. He watched her for a moment. He imagined her dreams. Words formed in his mind and he leant over her – that distinct, small-child smell – to whisper them softly. Sometimes he wished she was older. He was eager for the long conversations they would have.

On the horizon, or just beneath it, there was an orange glow. A new day was coming, it was just there, beyond the curve of the earth. All the hours he'd have to endure. There was a hand on his shoulder. It was Beth's hand. He didn't turn around, just put his cheek down against it and closed his eyes. She sat down beside him as the church bell rang again, chasing the birds off their branches.

CHAPTER THREE

Beth waited until Tim had left before going out to the bin in front of the house. She rummaged inside it until she found the envelope she'd thrown away the previous evening. She had buried it beneath the cereal boxes and tins. A bouquet of flowers had also been shoved towards the bottom; there it was, its stems broken and bent where she'd squashed it down. She retrieved the envelope and wiped it clean on her jeans. She looked around. The driveways were empty, all the neighbours had gone for the day. She opened the envelope and read the note again: *'We missed the first plane, but I've been brought up to think it's only polite to give a lady two chances to say no. Love Kyle.'* She rolled her eyes at the word *love*. There was a boarding pass inside the envelope too. She took both back inside the house, incriminating, incendiary scraps of paper that they were, and put them in her purse.

'Stupid girl,' she said to herself.

Upstairs, her new dress was laid out on the bed. She liked the purple and black stripes beneath the spaghetti straps. It reminded her of something she might have worn when she was younger, slimmer, more of the time. Increasingly, she felt now like she was being ushered towards the back door of the party. Turning her back to the mirror she removed her jeans and T-shirt. Of course, when she wore this dress she wouldn't wear this underwear; she had hold-me-in knickers and a push-up bra that told any number of falsehoods on her behalf. She made a mental note to allow for these concessions, and then, rearranging herself as best she could, tucking down and puffing up, she turned around.

Ah. Well. She'd been hopeful but, after standing at different angles and trying to be as forgiving as possible, her shoulders drooped and her body slouched. She greeted such moments differently each time. Sometimes they hardly touched her. She was older. The dainty, unfulfilled girl she'd been had been transformed. She was a mother now and in front of her was a mature woman whose body bore the inevitable signs of creating new life. But other times these moments moved her greatly. She saw in her body the years that had already passed, the layers that had settled on her and she knew she'd never again be as beautiful as she once was. Each day from now on it would only get worse and how could anybody desire this bloated thing? Most of the time though it was somewhere in between – more resignation than anything else, a slightly sad recognition that came with a question: *Can I still get away with this?*

'You look pretty, Mummy.' The little voice startled her. She turned quickly from the mirror and saw Ruby standing in the doorway. She watched the child waddle slowly over towards her and then her arms were wrapped around one of her legs. She looked down at the curly mess of blonde hair. Her hands hovered awkwardly in the air. The dress had no pockets into which they could retreat. Eventually, at a loss, she started to pat the child on the head.

She was three, this child of hers, nearly four, and Beth couldn't help but see herself in her, the nose, the sardonic, slightly strange twist to the mouth. Yet still she looked at her with wonder, not doe-eyed wonder full of pride and love and adoration, but wonder in the sense of surprise and curiosity, as in, '*I wonder who you are, and what you're doing in my home.*' The child would toddle into the room, as she had done then, and Beth would stare at it uncomprehendingly. 'Hello, Mummy,' it would say, making its way across the carpet towards her. She would see it coming, getting closer, and realise that she was its destination. It would clamber onto her, paw at her face, and Beth would respond by doing and saying the things she'd seen other mothers do and say.

Ruby arrived more than a month early. Beth had still been at work when suddenly a puddle formed between her feet. A day later she was at home with this tiny living thing that had suddenly taken the place of everything else in her life. She had read in books what to expect and how she should feel, but none of it matched. Instead, she felt disengaged, even irritated. Rather than some ethereal glow and a new, deep, otherworldly peace, she was pale and tired and her ruined body ached all the time. She spent the first two weeks in bed, spending as little time as she could with the child. But then Tim returned to work and she found herself alone with this strange person. It kept looking at her, trying to touch her. It seemed to be demanding something from her.

'I have nothing for you,' Beth said, shrugging her shoulders at it.

Over the fence she'd watch her neighbour manage a brood that seemed to multiply every month. One and then two and then three of them, from infant to toddler, clinging to her ankles while she waded over the grass. They wailed, laughed, screeched, babbled, chattered; all the time this constant noise coming out of them.

'You have your hands full,' Beth said.

'And they're all so different,' said her neighbour smiling heartily. She seemed to wallow in it. She chatted back to them in strange voices and made faces and seemed, to Beth at least, who stood silently watching with the wet washing soaking her top, the happiest person she'd ever seen. She'd go back inside to where Ruby remained strapped in her chair, gurgling to herself and batting the soft toys hanging from her mobile. She would kneel down and the child would stop playing and look at her expectantly. She would try to think of something to say. After a while she'd make one of the noises she'd heard her neighbour make, but it sounded odd and embarrassing and she'd fall silent again. The baby would grow bored, it would turn its attention back to the fluffy toys dangling in front of her. Beth would flick at one too, watching it swing back and forth, and then she'd get up and walk away.

For nearly two years she felt like this around her child. At first, she thought it would still come, this bond, that it had only been delayed because Ruby was premature and her body hadn't been ready and the maternal chemicals not yet produced and released into the bloodstream. But when it didn't come, not in the first week or the first month or the first year, its place was taken by an insidious shame she could never articulate.

'She's absolutely adorable,' the mothers in the park would say. 'You must be so proud.' Beth would agree that she was, yes, so proud, but to their backs she'd hiss, 'Sometimes I just want my life back! Is that so fucking terrible?'

It didn't help that Tim was a natural. It had come from nowhere. He'd never had any interest in babies or children before, and even during her pregnancy he'd acted as if nothing was changing, showing only the most cursory interests in scans and kicks. But from the moment Ruby was there he behaved as if she always had been. He hardly broke stride. While Beth was so terrified of hurting this precious bundle that she felt hardly able to touch it, Tim manipulated Ruby with confident carelessness. She'd watch him wrestle her, throw her into the air, change her nappy while balancing her on his knee. Each effortless gesture of his felt like a finger pointed at her. She began, inevitably, to hate him a little. 'You're a great mother,' he said to her encouragingly, more than once, but she didn't believe it and he didn't mean it.

Beth went downstairs into the kitchen. She stood at the sink watching the water slowly rise above last night's plates and this morning's bowls. There were three people in the household. *How could there be eight dirty spoons? He wouldn't have all that energy to play with her if he had to do this every day; he gets to be the fun one while I'm busy doing all the work.* She looked down at her hands in the dirty water. She hated the way the washing-up liquid made them smell, and how it dried them out.

'Mummy.'

If you rinsed a bowl immediately it made such a difference. But he'd left his on the side. It had been there for hours and the porridge had hardened like cement. She scratched at it faster and could feel the cloth sliding futilely over the corrugated surface.

'Mummy.'

She dropped the bowl back into the sink. She made a mental note to come back to it later, after it had soaked for an hour or two. There was something else as well, something else she was supposed to do, or to have done. She stared out the window and tried to remember what it was. Would he ever cut the grass again in his life? A school form that needed signing, perhaps, or more milk, or was there washing in the machine? She closed her eyes and took a deep breath. There was so much to remember.

'Mummy.'

'What now!' She spun round. Ruby was staring at her through wide eyes.

'There is a man at the door.'

'What? Who is it? Oh, never mind. I'll go.' She dried her hands on the dishcloth. One of Ruby's pictures was stuck to the wall with Blu-Tack. The top corner had come loose. That corner was always loose. Did no one else notice these things? She jabbed an angry finger at it.

The front door was closed but she could see a shape through the frosted glass. 'Yes?' she said, opening it. 'Oh my God.' Kyle was standing there. She slammed the door in his face. Behind her, Ruby was sitting on the carpet colouring in. She seemed not to be paying any attention. Beth opened the door cautiously and slid out through the gap, closing it softly behind her.

'Surprised?' he said.

'What the fuck are you doing here?'

They'd never met before now. Their affair, if that's what it could be called, had been conducted over the phone – through messages, photos, very occasional calls.

'You can't be here. How did you even get my address?'

'You got the flowers?'

She nodded at the bin. 'They're in there. What are you trying to do? You have to leave. Right now.'

'I will. I just came to say the flight's tomorrow. I hope to see you there.'

'You won't. Now go, for fuck sakes.'

'I'm going.' He glanced over her shoulder at the closed door. 'Was that your daughter?'

'Kyle. Get the fuck out of here.'

He put his hands up to placate her. 'Don't worry, I'm not here to ruin things. I promise.' He started backing away down the path, stopped, strode up to her and kissed her on the cheek. 'You're even sexier in person, Beth. Come with me tomorrow.'

Beth closed the door behind her. Ruby hadn't moved, and she didn't look up when her mother walked past her and disappeared up the stairs.

Beth wondered what Tim would say if he knew about her other men. She leant back, recoiling from the phrase. Her other men. It made it sound so tawdry, so much worse than it was. People would draw conclusions. There had been four in total. Three before Kyle, and then Kyle, who was the fourth. She'd known him for six months. He was younger than her, good-looking, although not really her type, and already much richer than they'd ever be. He'd recently been to Monaco and tomorrow was going to Reykjavík, the capital of Iceland, with a population of 140,000. It's famous for its nightlife, its volcanoes and hot springs. She'd looked it up. She imagined herself there, mixing with the young and the beautiful, being among them, almost being one of them, dancing her way back to their room in the small hours.

It was never a serious option. Reykjavík was just a case of *here's what you might have won'*. What did he do for work? He had told her, but she couldn't recall. Where was he born, did he have any brothers or sisters, what had he wanted to be growing up? She knew none of this. But she preferred that. The less she knew, the less real he was. The truth was that, to her, he was simply that magic mirror on the wall telling her she was the most beautiful of them all. That's all she ever wanted him to be. She knew very well that you went so far, playing these make-believe games, and then you went either no further or too far.

And yet. And yet she'd put the note and the boarding pass in her purse. And he'd been there, very much the real thing, just an hour ago.

Her other men. Until today she'd never met any of them, but it would make Tim so sad, if he knew. He used the same words to compliment her that they did, but they sounded different, domesticated, coming from him. How long had it been since they'd had sex? Weeks if not months. She told herself her lack of interest was because of Ruby. Before that it was because she was pregnant. She couldn't remember what she'd told herself before that. Tim had been ever so patient at first. For longer than was reasonable he'd been ever so good about it. Then he'd started making grand romantic gestures. When that didn't work he'd moved on to gestures that were more direct, even crudely, embarrassingly direct. Now he hardly made any gestures at all.

She got up and went to the window. On the pavement below a blackbird jerked its beak into an empty crisp packet before flapping away in search of richer pickings. Her phone buzzed again. She ignored it. There had been a time when each new message thrilled her, sent her scuttling to an isolated corner where she could indulge herself. Maybe there would be again. She touched her cheek where he'd kissed her. For now though, she wanted to pretend a little longer, that none of it was real, that he wasn't real, that instead, again, exactly like before, it was only that longed-for mirror saying only the words she wanted to hear.

She heard him come in, panting and coughing as he took off his trainers by the door. She smelt his sweat and when he reached past her to turn the kettle on he put his other hand on her shoulder and squeezed, leaving a hot, damp patch on her dress. He retreated across the tiles and she felt him standing against the opposite wall looking at her. His presence there irritated her. She felt heavy and imagined her flanks hanging over her hips and widening her. She turned around and stared at his bare, almost hairless knees. The flight to Iceland was late afternoon. She could be in a hot spa with snowflakes in her hair in little more than twenty-four hours. Would she even be missed?

'You look worried,' Tim said to her.

She looked at him now, tried to name what she was feeling and failed. They had been married for six years but had been together ever since he was eight and she was the seven-year-old girl with the boy's haircut who had moved in next door. She had seen him sitting on his front lawn that summer's afternoon, his toy soldiers spread out on the grass, and had walked over there. For a few minutes they had assessed each other without looking directly at one another. Eventually he resumed his game, but silently now, more self-consciously, until, and she never understood why, she stuck out a foot and kicked his men to the ground. Her maturity had overtaken his in early adolescence, her boy's haircut became a ponytail, and she waited two frustrating years before he caught up and kissed her underneath the trampoline. She wondered sometimes if it wasn't just a trick of geography, their marriage, if she'd not have ended up with whichever boy had been sitting on the grass that day.

'We should go away for the weekend,' she said. 'It would be good for us.'

'That would be nice. Where?'

'It doesn't matter.' She smiled in a way that she hoped would stir certain memories. 'Amsterdam?'

'I wish. But I'm not sure Ruby would appreciate it there.'

Her smile faded.

'What's wrong?'

'Nothing.'

'Tell me.'

'Nothing. I just thought it would be nice if it was just the two of us. It's been ages since we did anything together.'

'You mean other than having a child?'

'Yes. Other than that.' The corner of the picture had come loose again. Why did he never notice things like that? Why was it always up to her? It was right there.

His face lit up. 'We could all go camping! It would be cold, but it would be an adventure!'

She stared at him and realised he meant it seriously. Camping. From a dirty weekend in Amsterdam to that. How far apart they were sometimes. *I'm not even a woman to you.* 'Maybe I'll go to Iceland or something.'

'What?'

'You've got no idea, have you?' She brushed past him. 'It's almost like you're daring me.'

'Daring you? What does that mean?' Then, louder, to her retreating footsteps, 'We're not twenty anymore, Beth.'

'No, we're not,' she shouted back. 'And I'm glad you like my new dress.' A door slammed. The house ringed with sudden silence.

CHAPTER FOUR

For nearly a decade Ben's parents had ferried him all over the country. After so long each motorway now called to mind the images he'd looked at a thousand times – the adult shops out of place, the country lanes being overwhelmed by a bigger, busier world growing up around them, the lone houses atop hills. He'd grown up in the back seat of the car: he'd been the young boy asleep against the window who'd been carried up to bed in the early hours; the gangly-limbed thing with the breaking voice; the teenager watching the lights go by, thinking thoughts that shamed and delighted him. Sometimes he thought about his brother, who'd been dragged across the country with them until he was old enough to stay at home by himself. He wondered if Charlie, now twenty-three, had ever felt excluded.

'Break a leg,' he used to say to him before races. Ben didn't blame him. The time and energy and money that his parents had devoted to their youngest son meant there was never much left over for their eldest. He must have resented it. But the reality was there was very little about Charlie for even the most even-minded parent to invest in. Sometime before his teens he had discovered a digital world that he preferred to the real one, and very quickly after that the person who was just starting to emerge vanished, replaced instead by a sullen, insular being who picked at his spots alone in his room. Who knew what he did up there, sitting on his bed with the curtains closed and a dozen different devices flashing around him day and night. Maybe he had become a millionaire on the stocks, maybe he was a poker shark or a porn addict. Maybe he was all these things or none of them. Ben hardly noticed when he went to university. And he certainly didn't miss him.

It was different now that he had learned to drive. For the last few years he'd grown increasingly embarrassed to arrive at the track with his parents in tow. He was taller than his mother and stronger than his father. He'd walk in front or behind them, pretending to be alone, and then remain in the changing rooms a long time after his shower so there were fewer people to see them leave together. Eventually his parents began to withdraw. They no longer cheered loudly from the stands when he led down the straight, they kept their distance before races and waited for him in the car afterwards. Then one day his father handed him the keys and stood in the road with his mother watching him drive away. Ben had seen them in the rear-view mirror getting smaller and smaller.

Very soon after that their place in the car had been taken by Madeline. He remembered looking over at her beside him, her bare feet on the dashboard while the sun shone through the window onto her slender, freckled thighs. It had felt like crossing a threshold.

She only ever went to watch him run once. He pulled up outside her house early one morning and inwardly winced when she came out, looking the way she did. He was wearing a tracksuit, had been in bed by 10pm the night before and risen an hour earlier to breakfast on porridge and honey and sliced banana. She climbed into the car beside him and he could smell her immediately.

'All set?' he asked lightly. She ignored him. She lowered her seat and went straight to sleep. For the next three hours she hardly stirred. She reeked of alcohol and smoke and the T-shirt she was wearing was ripped down the side. He wasn't sure if it was meant to look like that or not. He kept glancing at her, at her coloured hair, at the tattoos that snaked down both arms, and the bright streaks of make-up that distorted and buried her eyes. Hiding in plain sight, that's what she was doing, he wasn't completely stupid.

'Close the window,' she said. She was wearing black leggings and when she rolled away from him he could see she had nothing on beneath them. 'It's freezing in your car.' *You should try getting dressed then*, he thought. He closed the window and she fell immediately asleep again. In the silence he asked himself a thousand questions. Had she even been home? Where had she been? The odour coming off this girl was starting to make him feel ill. He began to despise her. She knew about the American Dream, he'd trusted her with that most sacred thing and this is how she respected it. He shook his head. *Enough. Fuck her*. He'd drop her off at the next service station.

At the track people stared, they stared as she approached and looked back over their shoulders after she passed. It was all done quite openly, as if they weren't aware they were doing it, or, if they were, hadn't considered that she could see them too. He glared at them challengingly, trying to shame them into looking away, but it was like he wasn't there. Then he began to realise what it was; they stared brazenly because they didn't care if she saw them. Dressed like that, inked like that, parading herself like that – in their heads it gave them permission. It's different littering in nature than in a slum. They walked in front of the grandstand. Hundreds of eyes all looked down at her. He put his arm around her; she was rigid.

'Will you be all right by yourself?' he asked. She laughed at him and then strolled away.

During the race he tried to spot her in the crowd. Each lap he scanned the faces, growing a little more frantic each time. He was running safely at the back of the lead group. He wanted to show her his fast finish and impress her just when she thought he'd lose. There were three people ahead of him. He'd raced them all before many times and none of them was a threat. He was excited to show off for her. But where was she? His eyes jumped about among the crowd. It was a small crowd. It wasn't as if she didn't stand out. Nothing. He would take the bell soon. She'd miss it. But he couldn't wait for her any longer. The three runners in front pulled away. He wasn't worried. They'd gone too soon, wouldn't be able to sustain that pace over four hundred yards. He'd accelerate on the back-straight and take them there. Wait, was that her? He craned his head to see. Suddenly the three runners ahead all stopped. One fell to the ground. A fourth came past him. Only when he crossed the line did he realise the race had finished, the final lap he'd been waiting for had just happened, and he'd come fifth.

<hr>

'How did you do?' She was waiting for him by the car.

'Forget it. If you couldn't even be bothered to watch.'

They drove back in silence. It was dark. He was thinking about the way she had been looked at, the way their eyes had pawed her obscenely. But then why dress like that? If you make a cake expect people to want to eat it. And he was no different. He'd like to have said he was, that he saw through all that, but whatever else he was he was still also a teenage boy and it was exactly those things that had first thrilled him. He hadn't dumped her at a service station when he had the chance.

'It took seventy-five years for the telephone to connect 50 million people,' he said. She looked at him. 'It took more than sixty years for planes and cars to reach 50 million. Even Facebook took three and half years.'

'Great story,' she said.

'Have you heard of Pornhub?' *Are you on Pornhub?* 'How long do you think it took to get to 50 million? Go on, guess.'

'Just tell me.'

'Sixteen days. Or so I'm told.' He tried to see her face in the passing headlights but she'd turned away again. What was his point? He had one, or the grain of one, but he wasn't sure he was making it.

'So?'

'So, I guess people are just people.' They went under a bridge, passed a junction, drove slowly through unmanned roadworks that went on for miles. The roads were nearly empty. It was calming driving through the black countryside.

'I'm just a novelty act for you,' she said much later. He was about to deny it automatically, but he then stopped and didn't say anything. He didn't want to lie to her. It seemed important for reasons he couldn't place. The lights of a big city blinked to the side of them. He thought of all the things that would be happening there at that exact moment. Someone would be dying; someone in that city was alive now who wouldn't be alive by the time they got home. Someone else would be born in that same span of time. He speculated on the birth-to-death ratio. The population of the world troubled him. He had raced in that city before. It was a huge place that just kept spreading outwards. You reached the suburbs and then seemed to drive as long again to reach the stadium. Someone there would be having the best night of their lives, or the worst, someone would be committing a crime, or be the victim of it. Someone else again would be at a fancy-dress party, posing as a clown or a court jester.

'And I'm just a novelty act for you, too,' he eventually answered. She looked at him sharply. Then her hand crossed the divide and rested on his thigh, squeezing it gently and remaining there.

'I like that, though,' Madeline said. 'When we're together we're both out of place.'

'Fifth, though, Benjamin? Really?' His mother was looking at him with a curious, misleading smile.

'Just one of those days,' he said dismissively.

'But you've never had one of those days before.'

'Then I guess I was due one. Anyway, it's not about winning, it's about taking part. Isn't that what they say?' He didn't believe that, of course, but he quite enjoyed provoking her. She was a snob, and what made her worse than a snob was that she didn't realise it. Yes, she was quite right, he had never finished fifth and it was clearly a conversation to be had. But it was the conversation that would surely follow that one that he was bracing for. He wondered how far she'd go. He'd managed to keep her and Madeline apart for weeks until both parties had started to suspect it was deliberate, and then finally, unavoidably, they'd at last had the pleasure a few days previously. 'You look so... individual,' his mother had said. The meeting had only lasted two minutes and during that time everyone had been quite civil, amiable even. But Ben had imagined all kinds of sneers and slurs and had apologised on their behalf the moment they'd left the house.

'I like your father,' Madeline had said.

Tellingly, he thought, neither parent had offered an opinion on her after that first introduction and he was convinced that since then they had just been biding their time, waiting for an excuse. Fifth place was that excuse. He was surprised actually, that his mother had waited this long. She didn't normally have a problem saying what she thought, it was in fact something she took great pride in. 'I call a spade a spade.' How many times had he heard that? She thought it justified all her prejudices. But this was new ground. It was softer ground and wouldn't be as simple to back out of. Perhaps that explained her caution. But she was who she was, and he sat opposite her, waiting. *It's all about taking part.* What nonsense. His antennae probed the air, monitoring the pressure, alert to threatening pulses.

'It's a long way up there.' This was his father speaking. 'What, five hours? You can never tell how that drains the legs.' He was offering them a way out. His mother snorted.

'Don't be daft. He's driven further and won.'

'And your hip?' his father asked, trying again with what he thought was a simple get-out. 'Any pain?' It wasn't that he was afraid of conflict, just that it rarely improved matters. And the closer the combatants, the greater the potential for damage. No, far better to leave things unsaid, to let heightened emotions dissipate over time.

'My hip felt fine, too, Dad.' His father sighed and sat back in his chair. They were as bad as each other.

'So,' his mother continued, assuming a free hand, 'what happened then?'

'Well, there were fourteen of us on the start line. We ran around the track a few times and by the end four of them were in front of me. So, I came fifth.'

'And there you have it,' she said. 'Wonderful. You should write for a newspaper with powers of description like that.' No one spoke for a long time. They ate their dinner in silence. He wasn't hungry but forced himself to eat everything; he felt, somehow, that not doing so would have been to expose a weakness. Afterwards, he took all three empty plates to the sink and washed them up. He could feel his parents communicating behind his back. He returned to the table and sat down again. This wasn't over, hadn't even properly begun. He looked at her and raised his eyebrows.

'What was your time again?' she asked, knowing full well he'd not yet told her.

'About forty-five seconds down.' She actually gasped and looked at her husband in genuine shock.

'Did you hear that?'

'I'm right here, my love.'

'But forty-five seconds? How? Were you distracted?'

'What do you mean?'

'You know what the word means, Ben.'

'Distracted by what, though?' He was daring her. He wanted her to attack Madeline so he could defend her, so he could hear himself defend her.

His mother looked at her husband, exasperated, but he refused to meet her gaze, brushed a sleeve across the table instead, searching for crumbs, trying to sweep away the debris left behind from dinner. She resolved to go on alone.

'I forget you're still just a child. So, did Madeline enjoy it?'

Ha! I win. 'Yes,' he said. 'Very much.'

'Really? It doesn't seem like her kind of thing.'

'And what do you suppose her kind of thing is?'

'I wouldn't like to say.'

'You're doing a good job of still saying it though.'

'Well, when we met her I was a little surprised, let's just say that. And that's another thing, why did it take so long for you to introduce us? It's almost like you were embarrassed of us. Or were you embarrassed of her?'

Her husband got up abruptly. He stood there at the table a moment, looking down at his hands clasping the back of his chair, then walked to the counter, filled the kettle and turned it on. She watched him, they both did. They were waiting for him to say something profound. When it became clear he wasn't going to say anything at all she tried to resume.

'I mean,' she persevered, 'she's not exactly... she's... I'll just say she's unexpected.'

Her husband turned from the counter, walked across the kitchen and stood motionless, still with his back to them, staring out of the window into the small back garden. He had suffered a heart attack a few years previously and had been reduced by it in surprising ways. He was quieter now, he seemed to occupy a lesser space than before and when he moved he moved as though reluctant to disturb the air. 'I'm not the man I was,' he had said and she had touched his shoulder and replied, 'No one is.'

'We don't get badgers anymore,' he said now. 'They used to tunnel under the fence from that patch of scrubland. I've left water out every night, but I've not seen one in months.'

No one spoke then, and she looked away from him to her son. She reached for his hand and felt him flinch but she did not let go.

'You know her far better than I do, Benny, than we do. We just want what's best for you.'

Ben wasn't prepared for that. His blood was up, he didn't want to just let it go. 'And you know what that is, do you? Better than me.'

His father chuckled to himself. 'Better than I,' he corrected. He walked over to his wife and kissed her forehead, continued towards the door. 'The American Dream,' he said to his son, 'it's your dream. It's not our dream.'

CHAPTER FIVE

Madeline's room was at the back of the house, on the first floor. From the window she could see into three gardens. When she was younger she used to spend hours looking into them, watching other children play. Her bedroom door had a lock on it, but she hadn't needed to use it since her foster father had died three years ago. He'd died a slow, prolonged death that had blackened the entire house for months until one morning the noise from the end of the hallway suddenly stopped. She'd savoured every moment of his suffering and both wanted it to go on forever and wanted him gone. But the escape that she'd expected didn't come with his passing. The damage had been done and the thing he'd put inside of her would always be inside of her now.

She ran away six times. The first time was when she was seven years old. She spent the night curled up in the corner of one of the gardens that she could see from her window. In summer the flowerbeds on the edge of its neatly trimmed lawn looked so safe and magical, especially if you leant in close, like she often did, they were a faraway land then; yellow and white butterflies would flutter among the petals and she thought if fairies did exist that's where they'd be. At daybreak she crept back home without anyone noticing she'd been gone. The last time she ran away it was different. She was cursed with growing into a woman's body while still a girl, and had no trouble finding a bed to sleep in. She would have run away again if he'd lived, but instead she repainted the walls of her room, threw out her mattress and began the process of burying him again. Since then, each new face had been an attempt to blur his old one. She imagined that if she had one hundred cuts, or two hundred, or more, it would be harder to distinguish the pain of a single one. By the time she realised it hadn't worked she was scarred for life.

Madeline turned away from the window and knelt beside her bed, reaching beneath it for the small tin that contained her papers and stash. She rolled three spliffs and then returned to the window to smoke them, one after the other. The gardens were empty. Fine rain almost too light to settle swirled about in the breeze. There was a knock on her door which she ignored. This was her quiet place. There are always quiet places to go if you know where to look, or noisy places that can be made quiet. Madeline had been seeking them out since as soon as she could walk. 'Where's she gone now?' they whined. 'Such a nuisance,' they grumbled. She had listened to their voices from her spot under the table, on the windowsill behind the curtain, in the cupboard, perched atop the vacuum cleaner with bare knees tucked up under her chin. She didn't know why she ignored them, had needed to ignore them, knew only that being completely alone was as vital to her right then as breathing. Someone had picked up a snow globe long ago and shaken it in front of her. 'That's me,' she said. 'That's how I feel.' They thought she meant the character inside, but she had been referring to the glass bubble itself. The slightest tremor sent the flakes inside her into a churning chaos, and only complete stillness would settle her down again. It was only a matter of time before she let the chaos out.

She felt her body begin to droop as she watched the rain drift back and forth against the dark trees. She'd realised early on that she was beautiful to men. She hated that about herself. She'd tried to change the way she looked by covering herself up with make-up and then tattoos and long fringes and dark clothes and piercings and clunky boots and ugly habits. But that had only made her beautiful to different types of men. Ben broke the stereotype though.

'I won't ever lie to you,' he'd said to her once.

Many other men had said it, too, or something similar, but she'd not believed them. She'd grown used to people saying one thing and doing another. Her foster father was the first one. He'd started it. He said he wouldn't hurt her. But he hurt her terribly, and when afterwards she'd cried he was angry at her and said it was because she didn't love him enough.

'After everything we've given you,' he'd scolded, 'treating you like one of our own. And this is how you repay me?'

It had confused her because she had loved him then. Probably more than anyone in the world. He'd always had more time for her than his own children and used to give her secret gifts. But behind that love had grown a feeling which she was too young to put a name to. In the shadows it had grown and grown and grown and then one day she realised it was the only feeling she had left for him and she was desperately sad.

She didn't recognise it as that though. She mistook it for anger and one night when she was nine she had stood in the hallway outside their bedroom, listening to them sleeping through the door. She could hear him snoring and for a long time she'd remained there listening, letting the thing that was burning inside her become a furnace. Then she'd opened the door and tiptoed over to the bed. He was lying on his back, face-up on the pillow. It was a warm night and the white sheet covered him only to the waist. His arms were folded neatly across his chest, and years later when she saw him in his coffin she would recall this night, this moment, and think, if only she had been braver. On the bedside table a picture of them all – she hesitated to call them her family – in a frame beside a half-empty glass of water. She couldn't see the image well in the dark, but she'd seen it many times before and saw it again clearly in her mind then; the sunlight, the smiling faces, his arm around her waist. There were similar pictures all over the house. Visitors often commented on them.

'Oh yes,' her foster father laughed, 'it's a picture-perfect life we lead. Isn't that right, Maddi?'

He was always standing next to her in these photographs. No one noticed that. They say that once you've seen something it can't be unseen. That might be true. But it's also true that people can refuse to see things they don't want to. She looked back at him on the bed. His eyes were wide open and he was staring at her. She stopped breathing. He glanced down at the hammer in her hand and then back at her face. For a moment neither of them moved. She felt the weight of it pulling on her arm. He watched her for a long time and then a sardonic sneer spread slowly over his face. How she hated him then. He mouthed something to her which she didn't understand before turning over complacently and going back to sleep. She dropped the hammer on the carpet and ran back to her room. This was before there was a latch on the door.

She had told no one about this, not even when his worsening illness had finally put a stop to it.

'I'm dying,' he told her after the last time. 'I'm riddled with it. They can't do a thing. Well? Say something, at least.'

Maybe she would tell Ben. He would come for her in a few hours. He would find her disgusting of course, but perhaps he'd get over it. Maybe she'd tell him everything, in the spirit of full disclosure. A burden shared is a burden halved. Was that it? Her head tipped against the glass. She'd finished smoking. She slipped off the windowsill, slid down the wall and onto the carpet. There was another knock on her door. 'Go away,' she shouted, or thought she shouted. From that angle she could see the clouds through the window.

CHAPTER SIX

On Friday evening Beth and Tim would phone their respective parents, Ruby's grandparents – in name only, they sometimes said. Both sets had moved away. Almost as soon as she had been born one set then the other had upped sticks and scarpered.

'Out of arm's reach,' Beth said bitterly.

'And harm's way,' Tim replied. It was a running joke. Of sorts.

All that remained now were these weekly catch-up calls, a last chore to be completed before the weekend could start in earnest. They would gather on the bed, Tim, Beth and Ruby, they would put the phone on speaker so they could carry on with other things. Sometimes they would make faces at each other while they heard, half-heard, for the umpteenth time, about the state of the tomatoes, the bridge club, the character in the daytime soap they didn't watch, had never watched. Frequently one, or both, would wander out of the room. Sometimes all three of them would slip away until urgent whispers in the hall sent them hurrying back.

'Yes,' they'd say. 'I'm fine. We're fine. She's fine.'

It was never more than that. Their parents these days appeared content simply to talk into the mouthpiece – perhaps that did them a disservice, who knew? They didn't know them anymore, or, more to the point, their parents no longer knew them – and when it was over they'd sit on the bed and try to ignore the sense of irritation, sadness, of guilt, all of these things.

But why had they sold up and moved so very far away the day Ruby had been born, while she was still in the incubator, yellow with jaundice. It might not have been that exact day, or even that week, but that's how it felt. Beth, especially, suffered from their absence, and during those first confusing months of motherhood she longed for her own mother, for what she hoped her own mother would be.

'She never sleeps,' Beth said once.

'Spirited,' her mother said back with a chuckle.

'But I'm just so exhausted all the time. It can't be normal.'

'You spoil her, that's your problem.' Beth was then reminded how much easier it was with disposable nappies, how convenient a microwave must be, and two cars, and online shopping.

'It's not as simple as that,' she protested. 'Doing things quicker doesn't mean you have more time. It just means you have to do more things.'

Suddenly Beth's father was booming at her. 'I worked at the same place for fifty years.' She could see him in that stiflingly hot room with the curtains that never opened, glaring at the phone as if it were an offensive object, sticking his chin out at it. 'That was quite enough for me.'

'It must be nice,' she said to Tim afterwards, 'just doodling away the last scraps of your existence without a care in the world.' They had no idea how fast life had become, how tiring it was, how demanding. And why do the clothes they buy for Ruby never fit? And why are the toys they send always six months behind her development? They should know these things. Other grandparents knew these things.

'It's you and me against the world,' Tim said. But Beth had never wanted it to be like that. She'd dreamed of big families, of long, loud Sunday lunches that gathered the clan. 'Yes, but they've got to live their own lives,' he argued, but that magnanimity was false too, was just an echo of something that had turned into resentment when he'd seen how their absence had affected his wife, how she viewed their leaving as rejection, even at her age, and how that rejection had manifested as spite directed, for the most part, and because he was the only one left, at him. So, the Friday evening calls. That's all that remained.

'They've shut themselves in,' Beth said. 'The world has shrunk around them. They think they've got a quiet life up there. They're wrong. They've just got a small life.'

But this Friday evening was different. When Tim arrived home he found Beth and Ruby standing in the driveway waiting for him. At their feet were three packed bags. He sat in his car blinking at them. He was finding it increasingly difficult these days to follow things clearly. Some events raced past him and left him dizzy, others unfolded in slow motion and distorted, as though they were taking place underwater. His mind had started drifting. It wasn't always clear if what he saw was real or only vaguely remembered. Suddenly Ruby broke away from her mother and ran to his window. He opened his door and she climbed onto his lap.

'We're going away, Daddy.'

He climbed out of the car but didn't approach Beth, who was still staring at him from the doorstep. Her face was severe. It sharpened her features, aged her. She picked up a bag, it was his, and approached him carefully. When she was a yard away she held it up to him and he took it unthinkingly. Then she turned around and went to collect the other bags.

'What's going on?' he asked.

She took the keys out of his hand. 'Get in,' she said. 'I'm driving.'

He stood there still. Ruby was standing up in the driver's seat. It was nearly dark. A cold wind had blown up during the day. There was rain in the air. Beth was in front of him again. Then her arms were around him.

'You wanted to go camping, didn't you?' She leant in closer, so her lips were against his ear. 'I know you think I'm a horrible person. I'm not though. I'm just sad.'

An hour later they were on the motorway. She was driving fast, away from the roundabout that bottlenecked the traffic, away from the flowers, now dead, in the bin and the answerphone that was at that very moment recording the slightly disgruntled voice of her mother. Night fell, slowly at first and then in a sudden rush. Cars disappeared behind their headlights. The landscape retreated into darkness. In the back Ruby was slumped forward in her seat, head flopping at a ghoulish angle. She tipped sideways, folding like a rag doll around the seat belt.

Tim turned his head on the headrest, saw his own reflection, ghostly and yellow, staring back at him.

'Are we falling out of love?' he asked. He was watching himself, searching his expression for signs that would tell him how he felt. His words floated in the trapped air of the car. *So much hate for the ones we love.* The phrase arrived unbidden in his thoughts and kept repeating. He couldn't place it. He'd almost forgotten his own question when she answered angrily, almost accusingly.

'Well, I still love you.'

Kate Bush, that was it, it was from a song. He remembered the album cover with her staring out of those large, dark eyes.

'Am I too late?' she asked.

Years ago, before Ruby, before everything that would come to matter to them, they'd spent a week at the campsite to which they were now returning. It had been summer then, and early one morning they swam out from the shore until they couldn't touch the bottom. It had frightened and exhilarated them. They'd taken off their costumes and floated naked on their backs, letting the swell rock them gently up and down. Back on the beach, on the ribbed, hard sand, they touched each other in new ways while the tide broke on their legs and the seagulls squawked and swooped in pious disapproval. Tim remembered Beth's pale thigh, how rough it felt with the sand stuck to it, he remembered the taste of salt and not knowing if it was the sea or if that was how a woman tasted, he remembered her warm mouth after the cold water.

He hadn't answered Beth. Without looking he knew, in the way married couples know things about each other, that she was silently weeping. He reached across and put his hand on her leg. Beneath the denim a muscle flexed and then relaxed. 'You're not too late,' he said.

That night, as Tim and Beth backed out of the tent, Ruby put a tiny paw on her mother's arm.

'I'm scared, Mummy,' she said. 'Can you read to me?'

It was very late, but Beth picked up the book of children's stories and turned to her favourite, *The Little Match Girl*. She began to read.

'Most terribly cold it was, it snowed, and it was nearly quite dark, and evening, the last evening of the year. In this cold and

darkness there went along the street a poor little girl, bare-headed and with naked feet.'

'How old is she, Mummy?'

'I'm not sure. He doesn't say. Probably not much older than you are.'

'And so the little girl walked on her naked feet, which were quite red and blue with the cold...'

'What's her name?'

'What do you want to call her?'

'The snowflakes fell on her long fair hair, which hung in pretty curls over her neck. From all the windows the candles were gleaming, and it smelt so deliciously of roast goose.'

How many times had she read it, had Ruby heard it? She must know every line.

'Oh, how much one little match might warm her. If she could only take one from the box and rub it against the wall and warm her hands. She drew one out... a warm, bright flame... she stretched out her feet to warm them too; then the little flame went out...'

'This is a sad story, isn't it, Mummy?'

'Yes, honey, it's quite sad. Shall I stop?'

'No. I like it.'

'Now someone is dying, *thought the little girl, for her old grandmother, the only person who had loved her, and who was now dead, had told her that when a star fell down, a soul went up to God. She rubbed another match against the wall. It became bright again, and in the glow the old grandmother stood clear and shining, kind and lovely.'*

'Her granny isn't really there, is she, Mummy?'

'She might be, in a special kind of way. If you believe in angels.'

'I do. Do you?'

'It would be very nice.'

'*She quickly struck the whole bundle of matches, for she wished to keep her grandmother with her. And the matches burned with such a glow that it became brighter than daylight. Grandmother had never been so grand and beautiful. She took the little girl in her arms...*'

'Do you have to be good to become an angel?'

'I think you have to be quite good. But really I think you just have to love someone very much.'

'*But in the corner, leaning against the wall, sat the little girl with red cheeks and smiling mouth, frozen to death on the last evening of the old year. The New Year's sun rose upon a little pathetic figure. The child sat there, stiff and cold, holding the matches, of which one bundle was almost burned.*'

'Is that what happens, Mummy, when you die? Someone kind comes to get you?'

'I don't know. I hope so. It would be very nice to think we could always be together, wouldn't it? But you don't have to worry about that. Not for ages and ages.'

For a long time afterwards they laid together quietly, listening to the wind and watching the weak lamplight swim over the tent walls. Eventually Beth reached up and dimmed it. Through the polyester the fire crackled and glowed. She wondered if Ruby was asleep, and what strange things must fill her head. She was only ever really alive when he was there; such a sullen, inward-looking child when they were alone. She thought of the weathered cliché about one hand being unable to clap alone. For the second time that evening she wept. She wondered if she would ever really know her daughter, and if she would ever be the mother she so wanted to be.

'Mummy and Daddy are very different,' she whispered. She closed her eyes. Her legs were too long for the short mattress and her feet hung over the edge.

'That's okay,' said a small voice in the dark. 'I think you're the best mummy in the world.'

———

54

Late that evening Ruby would wake up. She would hear murmuring from the other side of the partition. She'd hear her mother giggle and then something else. She would listen carefully, trying to understand it. It would sound like her parents were passing something heavy between them. They must have put it down again shortly afterwards because it went quiet again, and she would listen to them breathing and wonder whose was whose. She would still be wondering that when she too was soaked away in sleep.

CHAPTER SEVEN

Ben was sitting on his bed, turning the letter over and over in his hands. It was creased where he had screwed it up. Fourteen lines, that's all it was. Just 173 words. He read it again. *Words are never just words, as some people like to think. How subtle and wry and treacherous they can be when they get together. An army of anarchists ready to rise up and overthrow worlds.* He scrunched the letter up again and hurled it away, watched it scamper off and hide, trembling, under the desk. *So you should,* he thought, *so you should.*

'I won't ever ask you,' Madeline had said, 'that way you won't have to lie. But I know you'll tell me when it comes.'

Time was running out. They were awaiting his response and they wouldn't wait forever. Maybe he could break his leg. That would make the decision for him. He imagined himself wedging a foot inside a rabbit hole and then falling sideways. The prospect terrified him. No, he wasn't brave enough for that. But if he could sustain an injury naturally... Why did he never get injured, like other athletes did? He knew some people who couldn't go a month without their bodies breaking down. How convenient that would be; a timely rupture or serendipitous stress fracture. He'd been hoping. He'd even stopped stretching, praying that a tendon might give up the ghost in protest. But no. His body, his finely-tuned, unbreakable, metronomic body just kept on going and going.

'It's your dream,' his father had said. And it was. It had been. He had chased it with all the unswerving devotion of a zealot, he'd been that unshakeable shadow following the sun. But now? Now he wished that winning races was still the greatest climax he could imagine.

Suddenly he jumped off the bed and strode across the room. He changed back into the shorts and T-shirt that he'd discarded in a pile earlier and went downstairs. His mother was sitting at the kitchen table. Did she never move from there? She was facing away from him and he stood in the doorway looking at her. She was hunched forward, a pencil behind her ear. An unforgiving beam of light slanted through the window and singled out a strip of grey hair where the dye had missed. A song was playing on the radio and she sang along quietly even though she didn't know the words. She always got the words wrong, even to songs she proclaimed to love. Ben thought it was deliberate, borne out of a deep conviction that she was always right and her way was always the right way. Suddenly she turned around and stared at him. 'Another run?' she asked approvingly. He pretended not to hear and went out.

He had no intention of going for a second run. He simply wanted to be out, away from things, from one thing in particular. He walked quickly away from the house, turned the corner at the end of the road and kept going. There were the gardens again. There was the front door with the banner still hanging. He glanced over his shoulder. It was following him. He turned around and walked briskly in the opposite direction, away from the park. Soon he was nearing the high street. There were more people here. He might get lost among them. He stopped, half-turned. He knew it was still there. He sat down and waited for it to catch up, to settle down alongside him. He'd read it so often – a hundred times, a thousand times. He knew each of its fourteen lines by heart. When it had first arrived he'd looked up the university on his phone, had imagined himself there, sauntering across the impossibly green lawns under a sun that, so the website promised, shone three hundred days a year. He'd read all about the coaching programme, the scientific approach to nutrition and the inter-collegiate meets. It had been made very clear to him that all he had to do was turn up and they'd make him into a star.

He leant forward and rested his elbows on his legs, cupping his chin in his hands. He studied the pavement in intimate detail. People were walking past. He looked at their shoes as they went by and listened to snatches of conversations.

'Yeah, but when she does kiss him she'll be shit at it.'

'There's something there. He's not sure what. I've got more tests next week.'

'Why is he just sitting there?'

He enjoyed looking through these slits into other lives, glancing beneath the Elephant Man's hood. People's uncensored selves revealed more in five seconds than their public masks did in a year. He secretly studied them. He sought out those tiny tremors in the skin where ancient shocks still reverberated, wanted to bear witness to the unguarded moments, when the sadness, the loneliness, the bitterness came out. He felt like a thief, but excused himself because he never judged them. Some faces had more of this and less of that, but each was cruel and kind and curious in its own way. He thought suddenly of that slogger in the park. Who was he? What was it about him that had made Ben give up like that? He had felt sorry for him, but it was more than that. *Guilt.* The word suddenly jumped out at him. Yes. That's exactly what it was.

Not sympathy. Guilt. But for what? Being faster, fitter, younger? No. No, certainly nothing like that. He revelled in his vitality. What then? Maybe in a past life they were... maybe in a parallel world he had... He shook his head. *Next time I see him I'll run him into the ground.*

He was growing cold in his shorts and T-shirt. The air was damp and chilly beneath the overcast sky. Last week it was still February. He should've brought a jumper. He leaned down and picked up a broken bit of tarmac, rolled it absent-mindedly on his palm. Feet were still landing in front of him. He was on the outside looking in. He always managed somehow to find the periphery. Even running around the track or the park; even that was the edge of the circle. When he felt self-critical he thought he was better at observing life than living it. He flicked the stone away and stood up. And what of Madeline's face? It hardly moved. The expression she wore was confined always within the tightly controlled parameters. But he knew better. He didn't know her well, not really, but those telltale tics he searched for, they lived lavishly in the corners of her mouth, beneath her eyelids, at her temple. The stillness she affected was fake, was just the result of muscles always straining to suppress, to conceal. He thought of a rope made taut by powerful forces. He began walking home. He realised, with a shock, he'd never seen her smile. He would tell her. He couldn't lie any longer. He would tell her that night.

CHAPTER EIGHT

It was 5.59pm. Madeline was aware she was awake. She opened her heavy eyelids and for a long time looked straight ahead at the pillow just an inch in front of her. Eventually she rolled onto her back and then sat up. A bright light came on behind her eyes and blotted out her room. She sat motionless for a moment until it dimmed and then disappeared to reveal the wall and the windowsill and the window. She looked around. Her duvet was crumpled at the foot of the bed and whatever had been on her bedside table was now on the floor. The ashtray had tipped over and there was a scratch down her arm that had bled onto the sheet. She reached down and picked up her clock. It was childish and cheap with a big hand and a little hand and a faded picture of Disney princesses behind a cracked glass frame. He would be there soon. He was never late. She liked that about him. It proved that he respected her. She put the clock back on the side and picked up her phone. There was a time not that long ago when her number had been passed around and scribbled on walls and inside toilet cubicles. Sometimes she'd answered the calls and sometimes not. Then one day it rang while she was walking home alongside the canal. She'd reached into her pocket and then watched transfixed as the handset sailed through the air against the blue sky. She watched the ripples ring outwards towards the bank until they'd all gone and the trees were again perfectly mirrored on the flat surface.

Madeline went into the bathroom and washed the blood off her arm and cleaned her teeth. Her short hair was matted and she tried to brush the knots out and then gave up. She began pulling the purple strands out from between the bristles and dropping them in the toilet bowl. She did that for a long time and then reluctantly raised her eyes to the mirror. The feeling of revulsion came back as strong as ever. Almost immediately she reached for the eyeliner to begin the process of covering up what she couldn't stand to see, while in her mind she was saying hateful things to the creature in front of her. She was eighteen.

Ben had learned by degrees how sheltered his life had been. He had always known he was an innocent, but although Madeline told him nothing of her life or the things she had done and seen, he was only now beginning to appreciate the depths of his naïveté. 'You will love it there,' she had said, talking about the club she was taking him to that night, but the way she'd said it had made him nervous. He had felt, and rightly so as it turned out, that he would be tested.

She sat beside him now, crossing and uncrossing her legs as he drove the short distance into town. 'I like your car, but you should hang something there.' She was pointing at the rear-view mirror. He shifted in his seat so he could see her in it. He found it so difficult not to stare. He wondered if he would ever get tired of looking at her. When they were alone he wallowed in it, gorged on her. A look, a word – he loved hearing her swear – a twist of the body or the shape of her mouth; all these things, any of them, made the breath catch in his throat. But in public it was different. Walking beside her required a certain level of defiance, and sometimes he didn't have the courage or the energy. Only two weeks previously they had been walking home when a car had stopped in front of them, all four doors swung open and a group of boys got out. 'What did you say about my mother?' They hadn't waited for an answer. Ben and Madeline had hid behind a wall until they ran by and then made a dash for it, rushing onto the road to flag down a passing car while the group stood on the verge swearing at them. 'I know them,' Madeline had said, as if that explained it. Which in a way it did.

'It's just down here,' she said now. They were in town. How different it appeared without the people and the cars and the bustle. He saw the place where he had sat earlier in the day, saw himself there again, with his bare knees and elbows. Such a glum figure, when he should have had the world at his feet. She walked in front of him. Her skirt was tight. His breath catching again. She turned down an alley that he hadn't known was there. Halfway down it a door was open; a block of yellow light cut out of the dark, a weaker imitation on the opposite wall. A giant form in the shape of a person stood in the entrance. The bristles on the monster's scalp tickled the underside of the cross-beam. Incredibly, the suit it wore was still too large. The form nodded at Madeline as she squeezed past, assessed Ben with mild curiosity, then quickly dismissed him.

'Be good, children,' the monolith said.

'Where's the fun in that?'

They were in a corridor. It was dimly lit by a bulb that twitched on the end of its cable like a body on the end of a rope. It threw shadows around them, demented gargoyles that circled in strange arcs and rushed silently at their backs as they departed. There was a thumping sound, a deep, visceral beat that came from inside the walls and up through a floor. They could feel it throb in their fingertips.

'This is the place,' she said, half turning. They entered into a living thing, a thing that pulsed like the inside of a vital organ. It was dark, moist, sticky. He couldn't keep up with her, that was the problem. He tried, but, unlike her, he didn't have inside him a great heaving beast that snorted and charged. Ben found a wall to stand against. She was with him. No. She had gone. He waited. He watched the sweating stinking mass bounce in front of him. The strobe lighting froze them in a series of twisted poses, like characters in a film that kept jumping on the reel; this one with an arm up and hand limp like a wilted flower, this one with head thrown back and arms wide – he thought of *Gallipoli* – this one leaning right forward, straining, staring at him. Ben tried to affect boredom, as he had done as a schoolboy when he couldn't fit in. He was too young to be here. Or too old. Could you be both at the same time? Madeline was there.

'No one is looking at you,' she said.

He felt they were, was sure his awkwardness must show through. She put her tongue in his ear and he recoiled in embarrassment, saw her hurt expression, grasped for her hand as she pulled it away and allowed herself to be sucked back into the throng. The wall was moist. He felt it wet on his back. Or maybe it was his back that was wet. This music... But they must like it. He tapped a foot and nodded his head, felt foolish and stopped again.

'I'm going to make it so easy for you tonight. You'll thank me one day.' She was shouting at him to make herself heard, almost laughing. She grabbed his face, spat, 'See? Who wants this mess?'

A man appeared behind her, reached round and grabbed her. Her small body fell back into his. She stuck her tongue out again and let him press something onto it. Ben was frozen. It was disgust and awe. She twisted loose and spun away across the floor in a blind, directionless daze. He wanted to leave, to get out of there. He didn't belong in this place. He pictured her life, and his with it, glimpsed the chaos of it. It made him shiver. Suddenly he longed for the solitude and silence of the track. Of his own footsteps.

'You need this,' she was saying. She was in front of him again. Her top was open and a bare breast was hanging out. She reached down the front of his trousers. Her eyes. What was wrong with her eyes? Giant glassy moons bounced about in their sockets. *Save me. Save me.* Who said that? Had he heard it or only thought it. He reached to hold her but she ducked away and vanished again. *This is fun. This is so much fucking fun I can't stand it.* He pressed his face into the wall. His cheek stuck to whatever grime had accumulated on its surface over the course of months, years. Where even was this? That grim, barren hallway with its bulb leaking desolate light. The music still screamed at him. He thought for a dreadful moment he might cry. A big hand on his shoulder, a man's hand. It spun him around off the wall.

'Your girl.' It was the man who had grabbed Madeline. 'She looks different not bent over a sink,' he said. He opened his mouth in a leer. He had no teeth, not a single one. His thick tongue flapped about in an empty cavern. Bent over a sink? What did that mean? Was she ill? There she was. She was dancing. No, she wasn't dancing. She was shaking. Or being shaken. That beast inside her, it had come thrashing to the surface. Someone touched her arm and she lashed out, lashed at everything, clawing and scratching the air in wide erratic swipes. People drew back, some were shocked. The toothless man grabbed her again, restrained her in his huge arms. He looked at Ben. She was screaming into his shoulder, but the music drowned her out. *No. This can't be right. This isn't me. This will never be me.*

Ben was running. The creatures in the corridor whirled around him again. Something clutched his ankle and he fell. His face flat on the floor. He saw the scum and filth that had attached itself to loose threads of a carpet wasting away beneath him, colouring it the brown of cloudy water in sunlight. He scurried on his hands and knees like a rat made mad by experiments. The thumping beat stamped behind him, a large suit draped in the doorway. He pushed past it and turned left, towards the light and the empty street and the cold night air and the silence. His ears were ringing. He was sweating. It was behind him. She was still there. He tried not to think about that. He began to walk, he knew not where. Away. Away and away.

'Ben?' That voice. It was her voice, but it was a little girl's voice. It was trailing him. 'Ben?' it said again. He slowed down. He could outrun her if he wanted. He could run and she would never catch him. 'Don't leave me behind,' she said. 'Please.'

He put his hand against a lamppost. Who was that man? *I'm going to make it so easy for you tonight.* That's what she'd said. She was behind him now. He stared in the opposite direction, at the black glass fronts of closed shops. He waited for her to do something. Finally, his pride gave way and he looked back. She was sitting cross-legged a few paces away. Between them on the ground had been placed a tiny plastic trainer, pale blue apart from white toecaps and laces.

'It's nothing really,' she said. 'I thought you might like it. For your new car.'

'Jesus, I don't think I can handle all this.' He leant against the lamppost and slowly slid down onto his haunches. The trainer was on the ground at her feet. He pictured the moment she had seen it on the shelf, saw her slender fingers wrap around it. For the second time that night he felt he might cry. 'Who was that man?'

'No one.'

She allowed herself to fall backwards. Her skull hit the ground with a thud that made him wince. She stared up at the sky showing in the gaps between the silent buildings. 'I hate him,' she said. 'I hate all of them.'

'Please don't take me home yet,' she said.

The pale-blue trainer swung happily from the rear-view mirror as they drove. Eventually they pulled into a lay-by beside the motorway and climbed up and over the verge. Fields of rapeseed unrolled black and still in front of them. They found a narrow path and followed it away from the road. The ground was uneven and he put his feet down carefully. Very quickly the sounds of the cars disappeared. They stopped and listened to how quiet it was. After a while she sat down on the hard sand. He sat opposite her. A million stalks rose above their heads, enclosing them in an impenetrable thickness. Nothing moved. The longer they sat there the more the stillness pressed down on them. From two feet apart they couldn't see each other's faces.

'You don't know me,' she said. 'Do you want to know me?'

She flicked the lighter beneath her chin and her face was suddenly illuminated in an orange light. She was staring straight ahead. She was concentrating. He got the odd sensation she was watching something. She looked so young. As he watched, her expression changed. Her face hardly moved, but the youthfulness faded and something else appeared that frightened him. He was about to reach out for her when the flame died and she vanished. The switch flicked again and he saw unmistakable terror. He thought of the bulging eyes of a wounded deer on its side on the road. Then she was gone again. The darkness lingered longer this time. When the flame burst into life a second time she was someone else. She was making a face, cross-eyed, puffed cheeks, head skew, but there was nothing comic about it. It was out of sync. It didn't look like her. The flame died and the stillness returned.

'No one is ever just one person,' she said in a voice flat with weariness. 'I know you've heard from them. You must have. By now.' She lit the flame again and her face glowed. 'So, when will you leave me?'

'Yes,' he answered, 'I got the letter. And I've been accepted.' The flame burned her finger. She swore and dropped the lighter. In the dark he added, 'But I'm not going. I'm staying with you.'

How big and bright the moon shone; it made the skin on her arm whiter than it was. She didn't go inside immediately. She pretended to, she walked to the door and then hid in the dark of the porch until he'd driven away. Once she was sure he'd gone she walked back down the path and stood on the side of the road wondering what to do next. It was cold, but she was too excited to sleep, and too hopeful to enter that house again. She turned to look at it. All the things that had been done to her were inside. Not all the rooms, but many of them bore ghosts, holes in the air where their two figures had once been. Imprints of those people would always be there now, trapped in the act, repeating and repeating and repeating. She would look at a chair, and in front of the chair, on the carpet or against the table, the scene, faint yet ghastly, would be always playing out. Even her room, with its latch and its view into the gardens, wasn't completely exorcised. No, she wouldn't go back into the house right now, not while she still believed that he meant what he said.

'I'm not going.'

'You're just trying to convince yourself,' she'd said, but only to hear him deny it.

'Just believe that good things can sometimes happen,' he'd replied, smiling.

She began to walk. What would they do instead? They had a car. They had driven to many places already and the next time they did they could simply not drive back. She liked how she said 'they' instead of 'he'. She sat down. She was still in the road but didn't mind that. She stretched out on her back. There was a drawer in a room that she had been in many times. She hadn't been back there for months, but she was sure she'd be let in again. Inside that drawer were rolls of £20 notes. She'd asked him once how much was in there and he'd slammed the drawer on her and pushed her back until her heels hit the mattress and she fell.

'Watch your mouth,' he'd warned, but later, when he was more relaxed, he'd said there was more than £2,000. He'd shrugged. 'That's nothing. More most of the time.'

She began to calculate how long £2,000 would last. They could rent a room, get jobs. Or she could get a job while he learned a trade. How long did that take? She began to laugh, imagining him as a plumber, bent under a sink or with his hand down someone's toilet. Maybe not. He could become a gym instructor instead, or a PE teacher. And once they'd saved more money she would quit her job and get a degree. Or she could study in the evenings. The question of what to study hadn't even finished forming in her mind before she had her answer, although she'd never once considered it before. History. She was surprised to discover that she loved history. She examined this thought a little deeper and realised she particularly liked finding out about subjugation and war. She wasn't interested in the politics behind it, the reasons and ramifications, but it was fascinating how cruel people had been to each other. It had nothing to do with the age, the nation, the notion of being civilised or not – all people, at all times, were cruel. It comforted her, that knowledge.

A huge roaring wind blew up from nowhere. A great blast of it rushed past her and then receded. She rolled onto her side to see the red tail-lights of a car disappearing down the road.

She guessed that it would take five to seven years before they would be ready to start their real lives. By then, all this would have been forgotten – not forgotten, maybe, but irrelevant; she would never have to think of it again, but if she did she would think of it as someone else's history. She would be Madeline the graduate, Madeline the taxpayer, Madeline the functioning part of society. She would wear long-sleeved blouses with the top button done up. She would have debates about feminism and foreign policy and cook Sunday lunches while listening to the radio.

Another blast of hot wind. She didn't bother to look after it this time. She stared up at the moon. It must be a supermoon, to be this big and this bright. Why had they not seen it earlier, in the field? Maybe there was cloud-cover then and now it was clearing. She smiled at the obvious symbolism. She closed her eyes. Inside her eyelids were the walls of her room. She gasped and opened them quickly. *No. Stop that. Focus.* The graduate, the taxpayer, the debates – she closed her eyes again. The walls were still there. She let out a short yelp. Above her the sky seemed very high and far away. Apart from the moon, there was a band of stars in the middle of it, twinkling in the dark space between the two rows of streetlights. She took a deep breath and then closed her eyes a third time. The walls were right in front of her now. *'Remember who you are, Madeline,' they mocked,* '*you'll always be her.*' She stared straight up for as long as she could. She began to see the walls even with her eyes open. Eventually she accepted what she'd always known and had only briefly forgotten, that she was the house, that the house was her.

She felt a tear forming and blinked, sending it rolling down the side of her face. She wiped it away roughly. *Of course he will go. Who are you kidding?* But despite that, or because of it, she realised she need never return to that house. She could just pick a star and stare at it, she could just stare at it and think how wonderful it was to dream of this wonderful life with this wonderful man, looking up, waiting, waiting and wishing for the wind to return and carry her away.

CHAPTER NINE

—————

For Tim and Beth, a day was coming. It would start with them kissing impatiently at the door and then walking out of it and moving inescapably to the hour, the minute. Behind them, in an empty house that would be emptier still by nightfall, a cup of coffee would go cold on the windowsill, a sock thick with dust would remain undiscovered beneath the couch, blinds would tangle and untangle against an open window. After this day they would scavenge among these things for clues that weren't there, had never been there. It would be the randomness of it that would make it so impossible to accept, that would leave them, in the half-gloom of a room that had darkened around them, staring at each other over the table in disgust.

Tim was at the nursing home. He'd not planned to stop there on his way back but his grandmother's phone call earlier had nagged at him.

'Oh, Tim,' she'd said, 'I think I'm on my last legs, and I'm so happy.'

She was ninety-nine and for nearly a year each time he'd visited her he'd wondered if it would be the last. On recent occasions he'd even found himself pausing in the doorway on the way out, looking back into the tiny flat to see her one final time. She was by now too breathless to walk them out. She would say her goodbyes from the chair that had been oddly placed in the centre of the room, and before they'd even crossed the carpet and heaved open the heavy door she'd be alone again, sitting fretfully on the shore of that black, black sea, listening to the waves licking higher and higher up the sand. Any moment now she was going to stand up and wade out into the dark waters where who knew what waited beneath the waves.

He wondered what it must be like, being on the edge of this vast, unknowable thing that occupied her thoughts so completely now. He'd felt it even while they'd been there. Large parts of her mind possessed by this thing that was so mighty it couldn't be ignored for long. What, in comparison, could he have seemed to her? Brief images flashing up from a reel that had run its course. Things left over.

She was born in 1918. She was four years older than Ruby when *The Great Gatsby* was published. She was a nurse during the Blitz. She was middle-aged when The Beatles were formed and already old when the Berlin Wall came down. She was sipping tea. His tea was untouched on the side. He hated being there. It was always so hot. Everything was dirty. He didn't want to touch anything. He compiled a list of things that hadn't existed when she was born. Televisions, toasters, central heating, credit cards, ballpoint pens, radios. Computers obviously. A world without computers. And mobile phones. Or any phones. The microwave, penicillin, nuclear bombs, spaceships. What would her teenage self, skipping along the hills of the south coast in the pre-war years, have said if someone had told her men would fly into space? And what else?

'I wish I'd had more sex,' she said suddenly. The pill. That was something else that was new. She said things like that now and then. Small voices from the ghost of the young person she'd once been. Her watery eyes fixed on him, recognising him. 'I mustn't complain. I've had a good run.' It must be lonely. To be a stranger to the people closest to you. Not the person she was. But the person she had been. More than half her life had been lived doing things that nobody who knew her now knew anything about.

He stopped again at the door. It was a strange sight, watching a living thing settle into a stillness as still as the dead things around it. The candleholders on the windowsill. The dusty shelf cluttered with photographs and ornaments that someone soon would have to sort through. The old radio tilting precariously on the floor, its aerial against the wall holding it half upright. He waited there behind the half-closed door. One minute, two minutes. She'd always been, to use the vernacular of her day, a hardy woman. Solid. Solid in a way that made you think of a thick tree trunk undisturbed by the storm raging around it. He remembered bouncing off her when he was very young. *Matron.* That was a good word for her. Now the high back of the chair dwarfed her sloping shoulders, and when he hugged her goodbye, he felt her dried out bones pressing through the wool.

He presumed she must be frightened. But she never appeared frightened. She was the last one left. Her husband had gone decades before. As a young boy he'd stood in the hallway late one evening listening to his mother sobbing uncontrollably in the next room. His father's low voice had filled the gaps between her gasps, but she'd kept on crying until he was too tired to listen. If Tim had been sad about his first real brush with mortality he couldn't remember being sad, and if his mother grieved longer than that single, fraught night he didn't notice that either. It was only in later years that he realised that there must have been many such nights for his mother, and it was only in his recollections that they merged into one.

Outside, he stopped on the path and sat down on his haunches. He felt like he'd been awake for a million years.

When he arrived home he entered a house that sounded unlived in. He wandered from room to room until he finally came upon Beth upstairs, sitting on their bed, doing nothing at all. Ruby was on the carpet in front of her with her colouring books. Neither had heard him return and he was afforded an unobserved moment to watch them objectively. Something about what he saw saddened him. Again, he wondered what would be left behind if he went. Only a week ago they'd been close. Cocooned in that intimate, blue-hued world of the tent, he'd imagined fresh starts and new beginnings and all other such hopeful things. But these things have nothing to do with where you are and everything to do with who you are, and he realised then, with the effect of something heavy falling through his body and landing like a new weight in his stomach, that they were still the same people.

He forced a smile. 'Ah, there you are,' he said lightly. 'I've been looking for you.'

They both turned. 'Have you?' Beth said. She pulled her shoulders back a little. He was looking at Ruby.

'This little lady here,' he said, kneeling down. Ruby was already clambering to her feet and she ran to him and jumped into his arms, making him rock back on his heels. 'Steady,' he said with a laugh. He held her out in front of him, staring at her seriously. 'We have a hot date, you and I. I hope you've not forgotten.' The child squealed in delight. Eventually he looked over his daughter's shoulder at Beth.

'Hello. I missed you today,' he said.

'You talk such rubbish sometimes.'

He put Ruby down and walked to the window. 'That man is still there.'

'What? Which man?'

'Him. He was there when I got home, just hanging about over there.' Beth walked over and stood at his shoulder. 'See him?' Tim glanced at her, then looked at her again, longer. 'What's wrong with you? You've gone pale. Do you know him?'

Beth's phone vibrated in her pocket. She put her hand over it to dull the sound. Tim was still looking at her and she tried on different expressions but none felt natural. He started to say something, then stopped and walked past her out of the room. She heard him descending the stairs. 'I'm going to speak to him,' he called back.

'Wait! Just leave it, Tim!' She ran to the landing and looked over the rail in time to see the top of his head disappear. She could hear him crossing the floor. 'Fuck,' she said. She turned quickly to see if Ruby had overheard, but Ruby wasn't there. The front door opened and she ran back to the window. Tim was crossing the road with that odd shuffle of his. The world slowed down, like in an accident. She put her fingers on the glass. The two men were speaking now. Kyle, standing casually on the pavement, almost a full head taller than Tim, was grinning. He was wearing a suit that looked out of place in this parochial setting. Something shattered somewhere. She registered the noise absently. She took her phone out of her pocket and quickly read the message.

Reykjavík is beautiful. I missed you, though.

Tim had his back turned to her and was looking up into Kyle's face. From this distance and height she could clearly see his bald spot. As if feeling her gaze on him, he put a hand up and touched it. She could break down now. She knew that. A deep well inside her was pressing up, waiting to surge, she had only to exhale and let it come. She pressed down on it. Suddenly Kyle pointed up at her. She gasped and slipped deeper behind the curtain. He stepped past Tim, who had turned to look also, but wasn't following. She could see him talking to Kyle's back. Kyle was halfway across the road now, still peering up at her window. He reached inside his pocket and took something out. It was a sheet of paper. Her mind raced. Had she sent him any letters? No. She thought of the boarding pass and note in her purse. She must burn them. But even as she thought it she knew that she wouldn't, that somehow she had to let this play out. Forests grow anew after wildfire. It couldn't continue as it was, whatever was to come after. Kyle, still holding the paper, stopped and turned around. He returned to where Tim was still standing and handed it to him. He wasn't wearing his glasses and she saw him squinting in that mole-like way of his. He turned the paper over a few times and then handed it back to Kyle, who folded it up and replaced it in his jacket pocket. Then both men turned to look in her direction.

Beth realised that Ruby was crying. She hissed at her to shut up. Kyle slapped Tim on the shoulder, not in an unfriendly way. Tim staggered sideways a little, but smiled up at Kyle and shrugged. It occurred to her suddenly that he must know. Maybe not the details, but he must know. The thought angered her. He'd said nothing. Done nothing. He worked himself up into a rage about missing socks and unmade beds and all other pointless shit, but did nothing about this. He was a fake, that's what he was. He was a fake, or he was weak. Or he was both. He was probably both. She despised each equally. Ruby was at her legs now, whining, pulling on the hem of her T-shirt – why was she so small, so impossibly small?

'What do you want?' she snapped, still fixed on the scene outside. Kyle's suit was navy. His trousers were tight-fitting and from the photos he'd sent she knew what was beneath them. She pictured it.

'It hurts, Mummy.'

Beth looked down to see Ruby balancing on one leg. She was holding her foot and there was blood on it.

'Jesus, what now?' she asked. A glass had been dropped on the kitchen floor. She sighed. She remembered hearing it. Ruby had walked in the broken bits. Behind her on the carpet red smears marked her footprints. Beth picked her up and carried her into the bathroom. She plonked her daughter in the bath and knelt down. Holding Ruby by the calf, she began to examine the underside of her foot. There were three cuts, two in the heel and one in the arch. One still had a tiny splinter of glass in it. None was very deep.

She heard the front door open and shut, and then his footsteps were coming up the stairs. She pulled the single bit of glass free and washed it down the plug. The footsteps stopped in the doorway behind her. She could hear him breathing. He was breathing through his nose. Her daughter's foot was still in her hand. She was staring at it. Her daughter was staring at her.

'She cut her foot,' she said to the slender limb in her hands. She didn't turn around. She continued to wipe and dab, wipe and dab, wipe and dab. He said nothing. She couldn't hear his breathing now. She began to wonder if he was still there. But which he did she mean? She wondered at her own mischief. She preferred to call it mischief than duplicity.

'It's okay, Mummy.' Ruby pulled her leg free and climbed out of the tub. Beth heard her hopping out of the bathroom. Still she didn't turn around.

'Get your shoes on, Ruby,' Tim said. So he was still there, just a few paces behind her. 'We're going soon.' She tried to gauge his tone. His voice sounded forced, thick, or had she just read in books that voices sound thick. He touched her lightly and she started. 'Are you coming?' he asked. 'I don't mind if you want to stay here. Take some time.'

'Really?' He didn't answer her. He must not care at all, not even a little bit. 'Yes, fine,' she said, 'I'll stay.'

CHAPTER TEN

She waited until the bathroom door closed and then she waited until the front door closed and then she waited until she heard the car reversing out of the driveway. Then she sprung up and rushed back to the bedroom window. The pavement opposite was deserted. She looked both ways down the road. He was gone. She freely admitted to herself that she was disappointed. She took her phone out of her pocket again but there were no more messages. She began to type. *What did...* She paused, then deleted it. *Where are...* She deleted it again. She looked up. He was there again now. On the pavement. He was looking directly at her.

He lifted his phone to his ear. A moment later hers rang. 'You're all alone,' he said.

'They won't be gone long. What did you say to him?'

'I just told him some story. I'm good at stories.'

'What story? Did he believe you?'

'I think so. Don't worry. Did he say anything to you?'

'No, not really.'

'And now he's gone out. So he can't be worried. He's crazy leaving you at home by yourself.'

'Why? Are there bad men around?'

'Yes. There are. Open the curtain so I can see you completely.'

She pulled the curtains open fully and they watched each other for a few moments. She saw his hand move over his crotch. 'Lift up your top,' he said. She shook her head at him. He glanced both ways down the road. 'There's no one here. Come on, Beth.'

She didn't move. She was thinking what bra she had put on that morning. It was black. Didn't someone say women only wear black underwear if they want it to be seen? She was sure that was rubbish, just another stupid male fantasy, but still her hand was gathering the bottom of her T-shirt and pulling it up to her neck. Below her breasts her stretch-marked belly hung over the waistband of her trousers, white and heavy like a carrier bag full of water. She pulled her T-shirt down quickly.

'You're gorgeous,' he said. 'Take your bra off and then do that again.' He put his hands together in a praying motif and then returned the phone to his ear. 'Please.'

She looked behind her at the bed, rumpled where she'd been sitting, at the chair that had its back turned to her in embarrassment. There was the pile of washing on the floor, there was the cabinet layered in dust, there were the photographs that hadn't been changed in years. 'Wait,' she said.

She put her phone down on the windowsill and walked into the hallway. She reached behind her and unclipped her bra, pulling her arms out through the straps. When she returned she lifted her T-shirt up again, then leant forward and pressed herself against the window. He pretended to buckle on his legs. He put his hand to his mouth and shook his head slowly.

Beth pulled her top down and picked up her phone again.

'Happy?' she asked.

'Semi. But who wants to settle for a semi?' He chuckled. 'Come outside and turn left. I'm in the silver Audi.'

She watched him saunter out of view. She was a little shocked at herself, not because of what she'd done, but because of how easily she'd done it, and how little she felt about it. She put her hand inside her trousers. She was dry. Maybe that's how these things happen, she thought, in an abstract, impersonal way that feels like nothing at all. She put her bra back on and went downstairs. There was glass to clear up. There were stains to remove. She went into the kitchen and turned the kettle on automatically. The corner of the picture was hanging down again. *Everything is coming unstuck.* She pulled the painting off the wall and squashed it into a tight ball. As she crossed the living-room floor she saw the small splodges of blood leading up the stairs. They would stain if she didn't clean them soon. She walked out of the front door and threw the screwed-up picture into the bin, then continued walking, to the end of the path, to the pavement, and then she turned left.

The driveways were all empty. The houses behind them were all dead things that knew and saw nothing. She wondered what she could use on the stains. *I will walk right past him*, she thought. *You go so far playing these silly games, and then you go no further or too far.* As she approached the silver Audi the passenger door swung open and she climbed in.

'I wasn't sure you'd come,' he said. 'Shall I drive somewhere?'

'No. I'm not staying.' His car was spotless. She ran a finger along the dashboard, felt the leather upholstery cool against her back. The engine was idling softly and the radio was on with the volume turned down irritatingly low. Why have it on at all then? She tried to make out the song. She realised sadly that she was still bored. Surely she should be excited, terrified, aroused. Anything other than this dulled detachment. Maybe it was because this, she, was someone else. She was still in the kitchen, scraping up glass, rummaging in cupboards. Now she was on the couch, scrolling vacantly through her phone. Where had Tim gone with Ruby? Had he told her? She was stupid thinking he'd meant her when he said they had a hot date.

She looked at the hand now holding hers, the thumb that was stroking her wrist. She could smell his cologne. He was wearing too much of it, it made her want to sneeze. If she let him hold her she'd take that smell back home with her. She became aware that she was being spoken to.

'But it's up to you,' Kyle was saying. She looked at him, grinning and groomed to perfection. How long must it take him to look that way? A vague picture emerged of her waiting impatiently outside the bathroom door, of him finally emerging with his face caked in cream. She would learn to hate this man in a week.

'What is?' she asked.

The thumb froze on her skin and his perfectly plucked eyebrows knotted curiously. 'Tomorrow? The hotel? You've not heard a word I've said, have you, Beth? Dazzled by my dashing good looks?'

'Yes, that's what it is.'

He smiled. She imagined a tooth glinting in the light. 'I'm there until Sunday. I was saying you should come visit me. No pressure or expectations. We can just talk if you want.'

'Is that all you want?'

'You know what I want.'

A car turned into the road and began crawling slowly towards them. She watched it approaching. She began, quite calmly, to think of a rational explanation for being in this car with this man. As it drew level she and the driver made eye contact. The car inched past and continued slowly up the street. Kyle was watching her.

'Anyone you know?'

'Do you care?' He made a face. 'What hotel did you say it was?'

He told her again. She knew it. Ruby was going to a party tomorrow less than a mile away. Suddenly Kyle leant across and began kissing her. She sat there and allowed it to happen. He was surprisingly gentle, and she closed her eyes and concentrated on what he was doing. She heard another car pass. Or perhaps it was the same one returning. She realised that nothing in the world could explain this away, and that she didn't care. She began to kiss him back. He murmured softly and his hand moved off her shoulder and beneath her T-shirt. She put her hand in his lap. Squashed beneath his trousers the blood was flowing hard. He began to move on the seat, lifting himself up against her. He was groaning. She withdrew her hand and pulled away from him.

'Beth?' he said. His eyes were glazed. His mouth hung open. She could see his trousers bulging. It annoyed her. No, it infuriated her, but she didn't know why. She opened the car door. 'Beth?' he said again. 'Beth, wait?'

'No. I can't. I have to clear up the blood.' Those quizzical eyebrows again. She realised he thought it was some sort of metaphor. She didn't care what he thought. 'This has absolutely nothing to do with you, you know,' she said, as she closed the door on him.

When she was back home she watched for his car to drive past, saw his face in profile as he stared straight ahead. She leant back heavily on the door. He wanted her. Everyone seemed to want something. But she wanted nothing. She wanted nothing that she had, nothing that she didn't have. 'I'm so bored,' she said. She heard her voice wavering. 'I'm just so bored. Everyone feels something but me.' She put her hand back inside her trousers. As she suspected, still dry as a whistle. Suddenly she screamed. She took a shoe off and threw it across the room, sending a frame crashing to the floor. That deep well that she'd suppressed earlier, it erupted now. It gushed upwards and streamed out of her eyes.

***

When he and Ruby finally got home later that day Tim stood in the driveway contemplating the house. He found his eyes drawn to their window. It was full of sky, white clouds scudding along on the breeze beneath a flat grey background. He imagined Beth up there, watching him. All afternoon he'd been anxious to get home.

'No, Ruby,' he'd said, when she'd asked to go on the carousel.

'Not now, Ruby,' he'd said, when she wanted to ride the mini train.

But now he was here something held him back. Things would change when he went inside. Things had already changed, but it was possible to pretend otherwise until they were said aloud. Ruby ran past him and in the front door, leaving it open behind her. Eventually he followed. Inside, he stopped and scanned the room, unsure exactly what he was looking for. It looked the same. Nearly the same. The patches of blood had been wiped into faint pink smears, the glass had been cleared from the kitchen floor. But something had shifted. Something had happened here and changed the air.

He spotted a picture frame broken on the floor, a shoe, Beth's shoe, beside it. That man earlier, outside their house, he'd been a surveyor, a realtor, an estimator. He'd sailed the seven seas and flown to the moon. He'd shown Tim the paperwork to prove it. He'd been lying – 'Your home?' he'd asked. 'It's nice. Cosy inside, I bet.' He'd winked then, or maybe Tim had just imagined him winking – but it was only during the course of the afternoon that he'd begun to appreciate the full force of the lie. He stared at the shattered frame, imagined Beth's back pressed against it, knocking it from its nail. He remembered the last time he'd kissed her, opening his eyes to see her staring at him in such a way that made him jump back. It wasn't disgust, or revulsion, or even hatred – nothing as passionate as that. It was boredom. He realised that now.

'Did you have fun?' she asked. She was in front of him, holding a cup out. He looked at it, at her hand beneath it and his taking it from her. He felt her searching his face.

'Daddy was grumpy,' Ruby said. 'He didn't let me go on any of the rides.'

'That's not like Daddy. Tim?'

He glanced up, meaning to meet her eyes, to challenge her; he thought he'd know for certain then. But his gaze fell short, it stuck on a vague area of her cheek – was it flushed? – and as much as he willed it not to, he felt it weaken, falter, and then wilt completely and slide down her body like a wet rag. She only had one shoe on. All the withering things he'd planned to say swilled about in his head. 'You're only wearing one shoe,' he said pathetically. He turned away from her and followed Ruby upstairs.

<hr>

Couples fall silent not always because they stop communicating, rather, they learn to communicate in new, subtler ways. Ruby was asleep. Tim and Beth sat unspeaking on the couch passing the remote control back and forth with increasing contempt; a physical expression of the argument they were not yet having. Out of the corner of his eye he could see Beth fidgeting, folding her legs beneath her, stretching them out again, sitting up abruptly and looking around before shrinking back into the cushions. She was missing her phone. He knew that. Normally it was an extension of her hand, but tonight it was upstairs, turned off. Silenced.

'So,' she said.

'So,' he replied.

The programme ended. They watched the credits roll. They watched the adverts. They watched another programme start. He thought of Amy at work, over whom he'd infatuated for years. She had put her hand on his leg once. 'Can I?' she'd asked. He saw again her slender fingers, her thighs beneath black tights. He'd put his hand over hers. It was his left hand. Orange light and shadow swept over his wedding band. He'd grasped her hand and placed it back gently on the table before walking resentfully to the door.

'Where's your phone tonight?' he asked Beth.

'Oh,' she said. 'I must have left it upstairs.'

'You never normally leave it anywhere.'

'I guess I'm full of surprises.'

Again she looked at him. Again he shied from her gaze. So meek a response. It appalled him. He wondered how his body had known to act in such a shameful way, even before he'd realised he was ashamed?

'I've got to work tomorrow,' he said.

'But tomorrow is Saturday.'

'I know. We've all been called in. At least you can have some quality mother-daughter time.'

'Ruby has that party at lunchtime,' she said, knowing the venue was less than a mile from the hotel. She didn't believe in fate. Everything is personal choice.

'You should go,' Tim said.

'Maybe I will.'

That afternoon Ruby had told him about a nightmare she'd

had. They'd been on a canoe, just the two of them. They'd paddled out into the middle of a lake and without warning he had plopped over the side and into the water. She had laughed at him as he floated beside her, just out of reach. He'd taken a deep breath then and slid beneath the surface. A moment later she heard him tapping the bottom of the fibreglass, *tap-tap, tap-tap*, before emerging on the other side, spurting water out of his mouth. Over and over he did this, each time tapping the underside of the canoe as he passed beneath it. Under he went again. A moment passed. Then another. She waited excitedly. She wasn't afraid. She trusted him. She began to look around to see where he might reappear. She took a deep breath and held it for as long as she could. She took another deep breath and did the same thing again. Still he'd not surfaced. Eventually she leant over and dipped her face into the water to try and find him. In front of her eyes tiny particles floated about in a brown, silent world. Beyond that, even just a foot beyond that, she saw nothing at all. She sat back up in the canoe. He wasn't there. The water all around her was flat and unbroken. That's when the terror came.

'It's just a dream,' Tim told her, 'I'll always be here for you.' It had seemed such an obvious thing to say then, and such an easy promise to fulfil.

Another programme was ending, another starting. The remote control was discarded between them. Neither had moved to pick it up. So much to say, but really there was nothing to be said. He stood up, dared to look at her finally.

'Just don't make a fool of me, Beth.'

She didn't even pretend to be surprised. 'Where's your famous rage now?' she asked.

'I'm going to bed.'

CHAPTER ELEVEN

The small child was hanging by tiny fingers. Below her, the ground seemed an awful long way away. Her wriggling kicked off a shoe and she watched it fall and bounce before coming to a rest. She looked up at her hands. They slipped a notch but held on. Behind her, her father's back was turned. She wasn't scared. He had said he would always be there for her. He had arrived over her bed earlier that morning, almost before it was morning, just as she hoped he would, when her wailing had filled up the house. It wasn't always him that came, but often it was.

'You're a hard taskmaster,' he said, but not angrily, and had lifted her out of bed and carried her downstairs.

Now they were in the park. She loved him bringing her here. He let her do things her mother didn't. 'Go on,' he'd encouraged, 'water won't kill you,' and she'd splashed down the slide, leaving behind her a trail through the condensation. It had made her leggings wet and the cold air against them as she whooshed back and forth on the swing made her shiver.

One thing her father didn't let her do was what she had started doing a minute ago. But he hadn't been watching then.

That other man had started talking to him and he'd gone over to where he was standing. She had sat down on the hump of a tyre at the foot of the slide and waited for him to finish, but he'd taken too long and she'd grown bored – bored and jealous. She got up and crossed the playground unnoticed. The metal stairs of the climbing frame were slippery with dew. They had lines on them, short lines pointing in all directions. They stuck up in a way that made her think of her grandad's tummy after his operation. She held the handrails tightly and put her feet down carefully, climbing all the way to the top platform before looking back at her father. He still wasn't paying her any attention. In front of her the monkey bars crossed the gap like a fallen ladder, like a dare. She put one hand on the first rung, and then the other. Ruby took a big gulp of air and then swung off the ledge.

Ben had a habit of being nostalgic for things that were not yet over. He would catch himself doing it, yearning for moments he was still living through, or for places where he still was, but although he recognised this flaw in himself he was, nevertheless, unable to commit fully to the present. He was in the park. He was dressed in his running shorts and shoes but was not running. He had taken a few tentative strides when he'd first arrived, given up irritably, and was now sitting atop one of the small rises. He wondered why he was refusing to run, if it was some sort of statement to self, an attempt to reinforce the promise he'd made and to turn it from a grand, chivalrous gesture (God, is that what it was!) into a physical act, a fact that couldn't then be unfacted. He hadn't slept the previous night, after the club and the field and Madeline's odd revelations and his own unbidden, unexpected oath. 'I'm not going.' He'd heard himself saying these words.

He had lain in bed watching objects appear in his room as

the light filtered in. There was the bookshelf, there the poster with the dog-eared corner, there – if he rolled onto his side – the letter in a tight ball beneath the desk. When he could stand it no longer he'd dressed and let muscle memory bring him back here. He leant back on his hands and looked about him, taking in the scene as if it were already a memory. There are places, ordinary places, that take on such significance when we're growing up, that resonate through the rest of our lives. Oftentimes it's only in hindsight we recognise them, but Ben knew already that this patch of communal land would always be with him. He looked at the overgrown tennis court with holes in the wire mesh fence, at the line of trees. Behind him, he knew, was the playground where he met her.

She was quite proud of how long she'd been holding on. It must have been as long as it took Mummy to make her dinner, and definitely longer than it took her to eat it. But her hands were hurting now. She had expected Daddy to have appeared already, grabbing her around her legs and pulling her away to safety, patting her bottom and calling her silly names. But he hadn't come. If she could have, she'd have turned her head to see where he was – what did grown-ups talk about? – but her stretched arms squashed her ears and pinned her face to the front. She could've called out, but that wasn't part of the game, it wasn't in the rules. She began quietly to count to ten. *One. Two.* She'd fallen off the bed once and bumped her head, but not very badly; the bed wasn't high and there was a big, fluffy rug on the floor beneath it. She thought this was probably as high as ten beds though. *Three. Four.*

Ben was surprised to see two figures already in the playground. He'd expected it to be empty at this time of the morning. He watched them for a while. They were on the swings. One of them got off and ran, tottered, to the slide. He stood up and began walking towards them. Halfway there he recognised the larger figure as the slogger he had seen here before. It was something in his gait, that same shuffling motion. He arrived at the low railings and stood there watching. Almost immediately the slogger stopped playing with the child.

'You need to lift your knees,' Ben called, almost surprising himself.

'What's that?'

'When you run. You drag your legs from your hips.'

The man looked down his body. His hips moved ever so slightly as he imagined himself doing it. He looked up. 'You're right.' He patted his thighs through his jeans. 'But my legs are heavy these days. It's easier to shuffle.'

'No, it just seems easier. It's not actually a very economical motion. It makes your legs go out to the side, and anything not moving forwards or backwards is wasted energy. Also, you increase your chances of injury.'

Behind the man his daughter – Ben assumed she was his daughter – had sat down by the slide and was watching them with a scowl. She was wearing pink leggings and a white jumper. She looked tiny compared to the big metal things around her.

'I'm already one big injury,' the man said. He was walking towards Ben. Even when he walked he dragged his legs, particularly his left one. It pulled his shoulder down slightly with each step, and Ben imagined he could see the bands, tight and short, resisting in their sockets. There were stretching exercises he could think of that would help. Suddenly the man stopped walking. 'It's you,' he said. Something passed behind his eyes. 'From the other morning. I didn't recognise you from back there, without my glasses.'

Ruby was very angry at her father. She was looking forward to letting go. She hoped she would hurt herself a lot, or at least enough to leave a bruise and a nasty graze. He would get in trouble with Mummy then. Even if it didn't hurt very much she would act like it did. *Five. Six. Seven.*

The man was talking to Ben about his numerous aches and pains. He looked tired. Old and tired. There was sleep in the corner of his eye and he kept yawning. It made Ben want to yawn as well but he bit down on it. Every time the man yawned Ben could see where his teeth were brown. 'But it's lovely this time of morning,' he was saying. *Is this*, Ben wondered, *what growing up does to you?* He felt full of something. He didn't know what it was or how to express it. He wanted, even in a small way, to make this man's life a little easier. He looked down and was surprised to see that he was stretching, pulling his heels up behind him and leaning one way and then the other. He stopped. He didn't want the man to think he was in some way mocking him. He would tell him about those stretches. They would help. He waited for a chance to speak. What was he saying now? He was telling him about his wife, who was at home in bed. He was saying that she needed her sleep and that, anyway, as he'd mentioned, he liked this time of day really. He dabbed a finger at the gluey ball of sleep but succeeded only in shifting it from his eye to the bridge of his nose.

'Everyone hates my girlfriend,' Ben said suddenly.

'Oh,' the man said, surprised.

'Especially my parents.'

'Oh,' the man said again. 'Well, it's just as well they're not the ones going out with her then.' He smiled, and Ben could tell he was pleased with that. He assumed that it made him feel younger in himself.

'They have their reasons,' Ben said. He hadn't told them yet that he wasn't going to America. He could imagine their faces, his mother's. He looked away from it. The sleep was still on the man's nose. He willed him to wipe it away. 'Her name is Madeline,' he continued. 'I like her name, but some people call her Maddi.' He looked at the climbing frame where the graffiti was. Suddenly his mouth dropped open and in one movement he hurdled over the rail and began sprinting across the ground.

Eight. Ni– Ruby was surprised when she suddenly let go of the bar before she'd even got to ten. She saw her open hands like two starfish against the sky. She could scream now if she wanted. The game was over.

She had still been hanging there when Ben noticed her, but he was still a few yards away when her hands let go. He lunged forwards and caught her when she was waist high. He was bent double and expected her weight plus his momentum to drag them both down, but there was almost nothing of her. It was like bracing to lift a heavy box only to find it empty. He collected her in his arms without breaking stride, trotted to a standstill and then placed her down gently on the grass.

'That was a close one,' Tim said to Ruby, as they walked back across the field. 'He's a very fast runner, isn't he? I can't believe he got there in time.' They were holding hands, but Ruby was sullen and she didn't answer him. She hadn't been afraid when the bar had twisted out of her hands. He had always come for her before and she had just assumed he would again. But even before those arms that caught her had settled her down safely she'd known they weren't his. They didn't have his smell, and when she had turned around and looked at the other face that was staring at her it had made her burst into tears and run past him to her father, who was still panting and red-faced by the slide.

'It's okay,' he had said, thinking it was the fall that had scared her. 'You didn't hurt yourself.'

He'd picked her up and walked over to the other man to thank him, and her whole body had gone rigid and she'd stuck her head into his shoulder and refused to look.

'She's shy,' her father had said.

He'd finally taken her away again and now they were out of the park and nearly at the stairs that would lead them home. 'We won't tell Mummy about this,' he said, but Ruby wasn't listening. She was scared. Not because of the fall, or because of the man who had saved her, although he did scare her and she wasn't sure why; she was scared because her father, for the first time, hadn't been there for her, like he promised he always would be.

Ben was sitting on the swing watching their shrinking shapes go up and down as they crossed the swells. He was rocking slowly back and forth, the way Madeline had that first time. He remembered her shoe bouncing along the ground. When he was fourteen a train had come off the rails near their town. Someone – they never found out who – had placed a rock on the line. The first four carriages had screeched through the hedges and toppled onto their side. Six people had lost their lives. Ben and a few friends had gone there soon afterwards out of morbid curiosity.

They had walked where the grass was still flat and searched among the broken branches for bits of debris left over. There wasn't much to find, splinters of smashed glass, a square of yellow foam with half a seat cover still on it. But while his friends had picked their way through it with excited glee, like children climbing over the rubble of bombed-out houses, Ben had moved off to the side and sat down alone. 'Don't you think it's weird that people died here the other day, I mean, right here, exactly where we are? Doesn't that make you feel a bit strange?' They ignored him, and soon afterwards he got on his bike and rode away as fast as he could. But that feeling of being so close to death had followed him. He had that same feeling again now. He stood up and walked to where he'd caught the child. Maybe if he'd not got there in time – maybe that's what it was. *What did her father say her name was? Oh yes.* He didn't say it though, not even in his head.

CHAPTER TWELVE

By the time Ben arrived home he'd worked up quite a head of steam. It was nervousness that agitated him. He wasn't used to letting people down and the prospect of doing so, especially his parents, created an emotion that looked like belligerence but wasn't. He burst through the front door and went quickly from room to room. The curtains were still drawn in the lounge. The back door was still locked. In the kitchen a carton of milk was on the counter and the stem of a teaspoon rose awkwardly out the top of the sugar bowl. The kettle, against his palm, was still hot. They were awake. Not that it mattered. He would have his say. They would hear it. He took the stairs two at a time and opened their door without knocking. They were sitting up in bed staring at him.

'I'm not going to America,' Ben said. Saying it felt like discharging a weapon, and the recoil jolted him back a step.

His father was holding a cup in front of his mouth, not drinking, looking at his son steadily over the rim. Slowly he lowered it and placed it carefully on the bedside table.

'Benjamin,' he said evenly, 'under no circumstances do you come storming into our bedroom like this. Please close the door behind you, and we will discuss this when your mother and I are up.'

Ben looked from one to the other, saw her hand slide over the blanket and nestle on his, and then backed feebly out of the room.

'Well,' Ben's father said, once he'd gone, 'turns out you were right, after all.' He squeezed the hand holding his, smiled a little. 'But don't be hasty.'

'Don't be hasty? Don't be hasty? Honestly.' She wrenched her hand away and was sat on the edge of the bed, pulling a pair of trousers up under her nightdress. 'It's that – that – that whore! I'm sorry. She is. There's no other word for it.'

'If you go down there now you'll only make it worse.'

'How can it get any worse? Oh yes. He's going to tell us she's pregnant, too.' She had put on a jumper and was leaning down in front of the dresser, looking at herself in the mirror. 'Good heavens,' she said, 'look at me.' She picked a brush and held it above her head but her hand was shaking too much and she threw it down again. 'I'm not waiting for you,' she said, striding to the door.

Ben was sitting at the kitchen table when she came in and sat opposite him. It was Saturday morning. 'Your father is on his way,' she said. She sat back in her chair with her hands folded, or clenched, on the table. Light glinted on her wedding ring. Dust floated in a slanting sunbeam. Last night's plates were in the sink and droplets formed on the end of the tap and then fell into the dirty water. She stood up suddenly and went to the kettle.

'Tea.'

'No thanks.'

A minute later she slammed a cup down in front of him and sat opposite. He watched the spilled liquid flow across the flat tabletop and then mopped it up with the front of his T-shirt. She glanced at him. 'I'm trying to be calm,' she said. His T-shirt was sticky against his stomach and he tried to fold the material away from himself. She watched him for a moment and then got up again and snatched a cloth, half dropping it, half throwing it at him. It came to rest against his forearm, and he slowly pushed it away and then continued fiddling with the hem of his T-shirt. He heard her tut, saw her through the top of his eyes glaring at him.

'I'm just amazed though. Honestly.' She simply couldn't help herself. 'What on earth are you thinking? This is what you've always wanted. And now you're just going to say, *pfft*, and forget it? The mind boggles. It really does. What are you going to do instead? Have you even thought about that? Because you can't stay here forever.'

'I'll pack now then, shall I?' It angered him, how immature he sometimes acted around her. He tried constantly to keep the little boy at bay, but he always found a way to undermine him.

'I forget sometimes you're still just a child. But you remind me soon enough. It's a serious question though.'

'I don't know what I'll do.' He shrugged moodily. 'I'll put a proposal together and then run it past you for your approval.' He'd not have said it had his father been there. He waited for her comeback, but she said nothing. In the pause that followed they heard his footsteps coming down the stairs. Not before time, he arrived in the doorway and stood there with a wry half-smile. They waited. They seemed always to be waiting for him to say something.

'You're not going to talk about the bloody badgers again, are you?'

'Are they back?' He wandered over to the window and craned his head against the glass, scanning all the angles. 'Seems not.' He sounded genuinely disappointed. 'I wonder where they are.'

'Probably dead in the gutter.'

He looked again out the window, this way and that, and then for a long time his head hardly moved. Eventually he sighed heavily. 'The sad truth is you're probably right.' He turned around. There was a cloud on the glass where his breath had been. 'Anyway, enough of that. I mean, that's just life and death stuff. What have I missed here?' Neither answered and he sat down at the table with them. 'It's the girl, yes? The reason you want to stay? Just so we have all the necessary information, do you need to stay, or do you want to?' Ben looked at him nonplussed. 'I'm asking if she is pregnant.'

'What? No. Of course not. I'm not that stupid.' He felt himself begin to blush. He saw her face above his, the bulb bobbing and weaving behind it. He felt his hands on her hips, trying to lift her off him, and her weight pressing down even harder. He remembered how easily he'd allowed it to happen, that first time, down there in the basement, with the cold floor at his back, and other times since then. His father was talking again.

'Not "of course not",' he was saying, 'not at all. These things happen all the time. And she does have a certain – what word do I want, mother? – a certain charm?' His wife stared at him.

'I thought you hated her?' Ben said.

'Yes, I know you did. But I wonder why you'd think that. I've not said a word about her. I suspect that says more about your own prejudices than mine. It's easily done. I'm old, or oldish,' he winked at his wife, 'and she's certainly a little... unorthodox. Of course, the world didn't have eccentric characters until about five years ago, so it's all new for the likes of us. The modern way. But we're trying to adapt.'

'Please, now,' his wife said.

'Sorry, dear. Actually, I hardly know the girl; you've kept her well-hidden. Probably because of those very prejudices. But the few times we have spoken she's been perfectly civil. Almost polite. Do you remember, mother, she said she thought that I looked exactly how a dad should look? I think she was making a joke at my expense.'

She was still staring at him. Ben could see her pulse throbbing wildly in her temple. 'What is this?' she said. 'You're on his side now?'

'There are no sides. We're talking.'

'No. You're talking. Or lecturing. Like you do.' His mother had a habit of bullying people by saying what she thought. Many people assumed she bullied her husband too, mistaking his long silences for meekness or acquiescence. But he'd never been a talkative man. He thought far more than he said, and although he'd been whittled down in his son's eyes from a hero figure to a small, ageing man, creased and stooped and fading, something of the Atticus Finch's still remained. Ben's respect had not diminished over the years, but shifted onto something else that was more real and enduring. He looked at his father now, standing pensively at the window.

'It's the worst time of year for badgers,' he said.

'Oh, for God's sake.'

'Spring, I mean. They have cubs. That means they must go further afield, cross more roads, to find more food. I'm sure I read that more than 50,000 of the poor buggers are squashed each year. Can you believe that? 50,000. When I saw that number, I thought of them all piled up, a huge, great mound of them. Isn't that morbid? And 50,000 killed – or "dead in the gutter", as you say – must mean 50,000 abandoned setts. Not all of them will have cubs in them, of course, but I'd hazard a guess that many do. Do you think they wait there, staring up the tunnel, or does hunger force them out? What a choice to be faced with; remain where it's safe and slowly starve, or leave the only home you've ever known and venture out into a world you can't begin to imagine, where who knows what nasties might be waiting.' He whistled. 'That's some decision to have to make, isn't it? A real quandary.'

He didn't look at Ben, who until then had been thinking that this was the most he'd ever heard his father say at once.

His father returned from the window and sat down again. 'When I came down here this morning,' he continued, 'and you were sitting there, and you were sitting there, at opposite ends of the table, facing each other, where could I sit but in the middle? I'm not lecturing, mother, but you did both make me referee.'

'You're so good at twisting things,' she said.

'It's the truth.'

'No, the truth is that what this boils down to is that he wants to give up on the chance of a lifetime because he's got a girlfriend. And how long has he even known her? How long have you even known her, Benjamin? You can dress it up how you like, but that's all this is.'

'We were his age when we met. Remember? Nothing would have dragged me to the other side of the world. And it has nothing to do with time served. You know that as well as I do.'

'It's not the same thing.'

'Maybe not. But we don't know that. How can we know that? Our parents would have said just what we're saying now.'

'So, you think he should stay? That's what you're saying. Jesus, I can't believe what I'm hearing.'

Ben stood up. 'Maybe I should give you a bit of privacy while you decide my life for me.'

'Sit down,' his father said. He sat. The wood was dark where the tea had sunk into it. He picked up the cloth and began sullenly wiping at it. 'All I'm saying is that it's not up to us. If he wants our advice, he can have it. But we can't tell him what to do. We can try, but he doesn't have to listen. Ultimately, what we think doesn't matter. It doesn't even matter what he thinks.' He looked at Ben. 'The only thing that ever matters is what we actually do. We are, all of us, the choices we make.'

The sun had moved up in the sky and the patch of warmth on the tiles had shuffled along a bit. Someone's tummy rumbled and they all pretended not to hear it.

'There are other scholarships.' The little boy within again, sulking and petty.

'Oh yes,' his mother replied, 'I might have a few spare ones in my purse.' She stood up. 'She's just not worth it. I'm sorry. But she's not. She's not good enough for you.'

Her husband put his hand on her arm. 'Hush now, mother,' he said softly.

She stared at him. 'But she's not good enough for him. You know it, too. How can you be so calm?' Her voice was rising.

'Come now, be kind.'

'Well, I'm holding you responsible then,' she said, before walking out of the kitchen.

Father and son listened to the footsteps stomping along the hallway and up the stairs. A door slammed shut and then the house fell silent again. Ben realised this was the first time he'd seen them argue. Maybe they had always waited until late at night or when he was outside playing. He marvelled at the self-restraint that must have required, biting one's tongue for hours without once letting the strain show. Or perhaps they had simply grown so familiar through the years that every argument had happened so often before that neither could be bothered to repeat it? Odd, that these people were still such strangers to him. He tried to recall the stories they'd told him and Charlie, about their own youth. There was something about a motorbike. Someone had walked up a path and punched someone else. It was his father who had thrown the punch. He couldn't imagine it. At whom? He seemed to think it was her father, his future father-in-law, but that was incomprehensible to him. He glanced up. His father was staring at him and he gasped. That wry half-smile again. After a time, he climbed to his feet with an exaggerated, weary sigh.

'Your mother was a fabulous dancer when we met, really something quite special. It was the first thing I noticed about her – the way she moved. Such fury and freedom. I was always too shy. She could never remember the words, of course, but the music, that was different. I wish she'd not given up.' He put his hand to his son's face. The son flinched but didn't move away. 'You mustn't be upset. Sometimes she means concerned instead of angry. It takes time to learn these things.' He smiled and nodded to himself, and then followed his wife upstairs.

CHAPTER THIRTEEN

B eth was standing outside the hotel door. Kyle was on the other side. She could hear the muffled sound of the television.

She had woken up that morning to see Tim standing again by the window. She didn't know he'd been up for hours, that he'd already been to the park with Ruby and was now showered and changed. He was in a suit but didn't wear it well. The shoulders were too wide and the legs were too long; they dragged beneath the heel of his shoes when he walked. He didn't turn around when she sat up in bed. There had been a time when his faraway moods had intrigued her, made him into something enigmatic, quixotic even. She had since learned it meant only that he wasn't listening to her.

'Are you going to that party?' he asked.

'I don't know my plans,' she answered evasively.

'Because I don't want you to,' he said.

Later, at the front door, he'd kissed her cheek and squatted down to hug Ruby. He'd held her for a long time and whispered something in her ear. Ruby had nodded and then hugged her father tighter. After she'd gone back into the house Tim and Beth had lingered on the doorstep.

'We take each other for granted.' Either he'd said it to her, or she to him. It was true both ways.

At lunchtime Beth deposited Ruby at her party and then walked the short distance to the hotel with nothing whatsoever on her mind. Any moment now she would back out. She kept walking until that moment came. Inside the hotel she looked around the lobby quickly to see if there was anyone there who knew her. A receptionist raised her eyebrows at her enquiringly, and she smiled in reply and hurried along. That took her to the lifts. As she arrived a door slid open and three people emerged. The lift in front of her was now empty. She saw herself in the mirror. She had put on that dress, with the appropriate underwear this time. Her hair was on her shoulders. Someone brushed past her into it and then turned around. For a horrible few moments they stared at each other in excruciating awkwardness until the lift door closed again and carried the other person away. Beth couldn't remember now if it had been a man or woman. She glanced behind her. The receptionist was leaning over her desk, watching her. She felt compelled to act somehow. She stepped forward and pressed the button. Her heel clicked on the hard floor as she did so. She stared straight ahead until the lift arrived and when it did she entered without hesitation.

A tingle ran down her spine as the door closed on her. The receptionist had known her secret. Kyle was on the fifth floor. She pressed five and then watched as the white light turned behind the number one, two, three, four. She felt the lift jar to a standstill. The doors opened to reveal two men. For an awful instant she thought one of them was Kyle.

'Going down?' he asked.

The question embarrassed her and she felt herself blush. He smirked. He also knew her secret. She stepped out even though it was the wrong floor, and walked halfway down the corridor. When she considered it safe, she returned to the landing. Now what? Immediately, she was faced with the same indecision she'd had on the ground floor. There was a large window looking out over the top of the town and she escaped to it. She remembered what she'd done yesterday, pressing herself against the glass in that smutty way. She remembered Tim standing up before going to bed, and the look on his face. She wasn't sure what she felt about that look. She knew he was a good man really, and that he loved her. She questioned whether she loved him back. She'd always taken that for granted, but here she was. She turned away from the window and found the door to the stairwell. A giant number four was painted on the white wall. She could hardly be expected to walk down four flights of stairs in these heels. She turned right instead and began ascending.

His room was 513. She hadn't thought she'd been paying attention when he'd told her, but somehow it had stuck. She walked up to his door and stopped. If someone came out of their room at this precise moment she would have to knock. In the meantime, she just stood there. She looked at her watch. It was 2.15pm. She had just over an hour before she had to collect Ruby.

'Oh, you're all dressed up,' the host at Ruby's party had said to her. She'd also known her secret.

One hour. How much damage could you really do in sixty minutes? She leant forward and softly laid her cheek against the door. You went so far, playing these silly games, and then you went no further or too far. This door, it was exactly that. She pictured herself on the other side of it, her dress crumpled on the carpet, her appropriate underwear discarded nearby. She saw herself on the bed with her legs up in the air, or bent over it, or maybe on all fours. She couldn't comprehend these images. They were so preposterous, outlandish. She lifted her arm and slid her knuckles softly, soundlessly, over the wood. *Now take your hand back, then tap it forward again. That's all it is.* Her hand fell to her side.

'Are you okay, ma'am?'

She spun around quickly. A cleaner was in the corridor. She was dragging a hoover and there was a trolley nearby.

'Is that your room?' she asked.

Beth tapped her throat apologetically. She didn't know what that gesture was meant to imply, and nor did the cleaner, who looked even more confused. 'It's just that I want to clean in there, if not,' she said. She yanked on the rubber tube and the hoover sidled up close to her.

Beth realised that she wasn't going inside, and that she was relieved. She pointed down the corridor. 'Just leaving,' she whispered hoarsely – she didn't want to be heard – before smiling again and walking back to the lifts. She didn't even like Kyle. Not even a little bit.

CHAPTER FOURTEEN

At 3.02pm Ben snatched up his car keys. The sudden rattle disturbing the quiet room. The letter screwed up in a ball beneath his desk. The door closing on it. At the foot of the stairs he avoided meeting his mother's eyes.

'Just off to Maddy's,' he said in a casual voice that sounded fake even to him.

He felt her eyes on him as he walked down the drive. It made him walk awkwardly, like you do on stage. He didn't want to be seen. The white Astra had 90,000 miles on the clock. It had a slow puncture in the front left tyre. On the window a thin strip of tape remained from an old parking ticket. He got in. The passenger seat was empty beside him and it probably would be from now on. He was incredibly hot. His skin prickled beneath his shirt and a bead of sweat tickled his temple. He glanced in the rear-view mirror, from which the small plastic trainer dangled by a lace. He turned the ignition and reversed out onto the quiet road. His mother's figure was still motionless in the doorway. He refused to acknowledge her. He put it into first and lifted his foot off the clutch, jolting the car forward. The small plastic trainer danced and kicked in his peripheral vision.

He'd had the conversation before, the conversation he was now heading towards. It had repeated in his mind hundreds of times since the letter had arrived. Sometimes it ended less badly than other times, but it never ended well. The thing to remember was to keep going. Sometimes when he ran he wanted to stop. *The finish line doesn't come to meet you*, he'd say to himself over and over.

It was only a short distance to the park, less than two miles. He passed the supermarket and drove through the amber lights. He passed the jumble of street signs that no one noticed and the tennis courts that were always deserted at this time of year. Further on, the tall houses without front lawns leaned over the pavement to funnel him forwards, the car's white reflection sliding over their triple-glazed windows. Up ahead, the green of the trees rose above the rooftops. He could drive past. He could turn around. He could simply stop. The thing to remember was to keep going. *The finish line doesn't come to meet you*. It was 3.11pm.

She crested the small rise and saw him sitting alone on the bench about a hundred metres away. She had read his message earlier that day – *Can we talk?* – like she'd read it a hundred times before. A single strand of hope had still dangled, but when she saw him sitting there it snapped like all the others and by the time she reached him the places inside her that had begun to soften with him had crusted over again. He looked up when she arrived and the expression in his eyes had no impact on her. She sat down on the bench next to him and waited. He didn't speak for a long time.

Eventually he said, 'I've practised this so many times but it's not the same in person.' She was listening, but from a long, long way away. She lit a cigarette and continued waiting.

'I told my parents I wasn't going,' he went on. He looked at her for a reaction but there was none. He said many things after that but none of them out loud and after a long while he put his hand on her knee. She left it there but it had no impact on her. Silence poured into the gap between them and forced them further apart. He withdrew his hand. 'But I've got to go,' he said. For the first time she looked at him. Her eyes were cloudy with make-up and difficult to see clearly. 'To America, I mean,' he added clumsily.

She looked away again and shrugged. 'Okay, Hamlet. What a shock.' She continued smoking, staring out over the wide green field. A line of trees split it down the middle. They were still in the calm, cool air. Beneath their thick plumage their branches would harbour nests and new life would emerge in the coming weeks. Broken shells would lie on the ground and downy feathers would turn over and scatter when the breeze got up. 'Was that all, then?' she asked, standing up.

His head dropped and his spine seemed to sink between his shoulder blades. He was hot again. On the ground beneath his feet pine needles had dried brown. 'I don't want to go,' he said. 'I've always wanted to and now I don't want to anymore.'

'Yes, you do. You'll be fine.'

He glanced up. The low sun behind her created a shimmering, golden aura. He knew what was beneath her clothes. He wanted to kiss her. 'And you?' he asked.

She laughed shortly and looked at him with amusement. 'What do you care?' She saw the shock and hurt come to his face, but it had no impact on her. She dropped her cigarette and watched the red tip go grey.

'You know I do.'

'Words,' she said, lifting her hand almost imperceptibly as if to brush his remark away. She reached into her pocket for another cigarette, but the pack was empty. She squashed it in her fist. Her hand closed and reclosed on it until it was as small and tight a bundle as she could make it. A toddler with its mother passed them on the way to the playground. She watched him until something in her gaze made it cry.

'It's not just words,' he said, but she ignored him. She looked bored. In a moment she'd be gone and this tepid, phony ending would be over. He felt short-changed. But he could think of nothing that would keep her there. *The finish line doesn't come to meet you.* He stood up. 'I leave in two weeks. I'll be back again in the summer. If you wanted we could...'

She shook her head.

'No,' he agreed. 'Silly idea.' She took out her phone and he saw her delete his name from her list of contacts. She began then to scroll through her gallery and he looked away, into the park. The graffiti was still legible. From where he sat he could only see a few letters, but he knew what it said. He found himself pointing to it. 'That's you, isn't it, Madeline?'

She looked up and followed his finger, had already known what he was pointing at. Playgrounds always appeared different after dark. She remembered her knees on the soft rubber that was meant to stop people getting hurt. She heard again the other boys' laughter echoing beneath the metal roof. Some were waiting their turn. Some were carrying on without her. She remembered taking the small transparent bag that was wet and sticky on the outside. She looked back at Ben. His face was ashen and ashamed but it had no impact on her. She watched it become a carousel of other faces, sneering faces, sweating faces, faces with blue eyes and brown eyes and green eyes and closed eyes and wide eyes that were glazed over, faces with thin lips and yellow teeth and broken noses, young faces covered in pimples, old faces hidden by white beards and dark glasses, fat faces, ugly faces, handsome faces, faces from magazines, from schoolyards, from dark corners and public toilets. Each one blurred into the next until they all became the face of her dead foster father, and then even his face vanished into a black and nameless silhouette in the glare of the bare lightbulb behind his head.

'I'm sorry,' Ben was saying to her now, repeating the phrase like he meant it. He'd told her once that he'd not lie to her. She looked at him, his earnest, guilty face. He affected concern and tenderness, but he was the same as the rest; rosy-cheeked, clean cut, kind-hearted, but he was just the same as the rest.

'Yes,' she said. 'That's me. That's exactly who I am.'

In years to come she would regret that. There would be another man there by then, and another one after that and after that. They would all be the same man. Sagging and stale on the couch beside her. A baby would crawl past on the thin carpet in front of the television. Another would be growing inside her. She would ignore those vague, incoherent utterances left over from last night's drinking and that morning's fighting and continue painting her nails. She'd wonder if things could have turned out differently. She'd see him walking to his car, his fine, smooth stride, and think of all the moments she still had then to call him back. She'd remember how he stopped and looked at her, and how she turned her back on him and walked away. She'd wish she'd been kinder.

CHAPTER FIFTEEN

By late afternoon the sun had baked off the early chill and filled the day with yellows and vivid greens. Puffs of cloud hung unmoving in the sky and dark shadows lulled beneath the trees. It was the first, unmistakable sign of spring.

Beth, bent forward at the hips, arms fixed straight in front of her, marched through the streets with Ruby regal in her pushchair. She might have paused to tell her daughter that three years and seven months was far too old to still require such a thing. But making her walk meant impatience, aggravation, avoiding the cracks in the pavement and picking up dropped things.

It was nearly 4pm when they began to make their way down the steady slope that led out of the centre of town and towards their home. It wasn't much more than a fifteen-minute walk. The shopping had been placed in the netted hold beneath the pushchair. Ruby was wriggling in her seat. A hard edge of something was jutting up painfully into her lower back. The bags leaned to one side creating an imbalance that pulled at the handles. Beth thought the milk had probably toppled over.

'Mummy, it's still there.' Ruby arched and twisted around to look up at her mother. She was put out. She was tired from the party and her voice was half whine, half reproach. She had already complained twice about the object poking her. Beth considered stopping. Had she done so everything would have been thirty seconds out of sync. But it wasn't far.

'We're nearly home,' she said.

To a bird flying overhead, the scene below was banal, innocuous, nothing out of the ordinary. There was no commotion, no drama, no sense of excitement or foreboding. It was just a quiet town, like any of the dozen or so towns it would fly over that day, with the to'ers and fro'ers toing and froing, the same as they ever did on a middling to fine day in early spring. Tomorrow, to that same bird or another one, it would be the same again. There would be no signs of what was about to occur. It would have been cleared up and other people would walk the pavements, other cars would glint at the lights. In a month, April showers would wash away all traces and then the summer would come and more people and more cars, and then winter and maybe snow, and by this time next year, at this time and on this day, that bird overhead would turn its twitching eyes down and everything would be exactly as it was, as it would always be. It's a strange, consoling thing, the ceaseless forward movement of the world. It means everything passes and nothing matters. We are, each of us, just pebbles tossed in the torrent. It was 4:01pm.

Barely a mile away Ben heard the heavy playground gate bang against its metal frame. Somewhere far off a dog barked in response. When he realised Madeline wasn't going to turn around he opened the car door and got in. For a minute or more he sat motionless behind the wheel, the keys in his hands and his hands in his lap. He watched her until she disappeared and then he watched the place where he'd last seen her, a small black shape that could have been anything, before eventually starting the engine.

He would replay the next few minutes of his life over and over again. They would be the dividing line that cleaved his existence into two separate parts. He'd see the dark shadows of the tall trees on the road and the light that flashed across his windscreen whenever he emerged from them. He'd see the yellow car veering suddenly and the driver's surprised and then angry face as she shouted at him. He'd have a vague sense that he was in the wrong. He'd see the red kite looking down from the telegraph wire and the old couple leaning on each other as they ambled along the pavement towards the supermarket. He'd remember passing the bus stop and the small crowd huddled within it, and the two boys on bikes who zipped in front of him and were gone before he'd even properly seen them. He noticed none of these things at the time, but each subsequent recollection would come back fuller. He'd remember all his thoughts crowding into his head at once, a single baying, swelling mob shoving out from the inside, each fighting for his attention and each just adding to the mayhem. He'd remember approaching the corner a little too quickly and how the steering wheel had wrenched in his hands and the instantaneous realisation that something bad was happening. He would never be able to recall exactly what happened next, although it would be told to him, but he would remember sitting in his car a split-second later knowing that the bad thing that was happening had already happened.

Beth didn't so much see the car that hit the pushchair as feel it. One moment she was striding along the pavement, opposite the bus stop, contemplating – what had she been contemplating? She'd never know – and the next a great jarring force was shuddering up her forearms, ripping the plastic handles out of her grasp and sending her spinning sideways and backwards, like one of those wooden tops she used to play with when she had been Ruby's age. But even before she landed, even before this sudden violent energy had passed through her and dumped her down on her backside away from the road, she had registered the horror of what was coming. It wasn't just the horror of what she'd see next, although that would be horrific enough, but, as well, it was the horror of knowing that this had just started, had only just started, and that from this moment on it would only grow more awful, more ghastly and obscene, and that she would never be released from its torment.

The car was not moving. Ben could hear nothing apart from a *tap, tap, tap* which was coming from inside the car. He looked up and saw the plastic trainer swinging back and forth against the windscreen. He wondered how the windscreen had been cracked. Directly in front of the car was a wire mesh fence held up by cement pillars and on the other side of that was a brick building which he knew was the electric substation. He saw that the front of his car had wrapped around one of the cement pillars and smoke was drifting up through the bent metal. He reached up and stilled the plastic trainer. As he did so he saw in the rear-view mirror a man running across the road. Behind him people had stopped walking. Some were looking in his direction. Most were looking at something else. A dog strained against a leash. A woman put down her shopping and put her hands over the eyes of a young boy. A second person ran past.

Ben opened the car door to get out but a weight against his legs pinned him in place. He glanced down and saw that the steering-wheel column was pressing against him. He reached down and slid his seat back on the rollers and as he did so the key in the ignition was dislodged from the hole it had made in his right knee. As he moved backwards a torn thread mixed with something else stretched between the two points until he broke it with his hand. He realised a man was leaning down saying something to him. His mouth was moving very fast. He seemed agitated. His tie was tucked into his belt. After a minute the man disappeared again and Ben got out of the car to follow him. His legs wouldn't hold his weight and he collapsed to the ground. Through the silence he heard a sharp snapping sound but he felt nothing. Using the open door to support his weight he climbed to his feet again. People were still standing on the opposite side of the road, only there were more of them now. The woman who held her hands over the boy's eyes was crying. No one was looking at him anymore. He followed their eyes and saw a mangled pushchair lying on its side, half in the gutter and half on the pavement. A thick bundle of blankets had been thrown from it. Two men were standing nearby. They were on their phones but both were looking down at a woman who was crouched over the bundle. She was bent so low that her brown hair hung on the ground. One of the men put his phone away and touched her on the shoulder. The other man said something to him and he stepped back again. Eventually the woman sat back on the kerb and looked up at the sky. Ben had never seen such an expression on a person's face before. She cradled the thick bundle in her arms, rocking it from side to side. Ben looked closer. From beneath the blankets, almost lost in the creases of her coat and almost too shocking for the eye to accept, two small stockinged feet flopped loosely in the cold air.

It was 4.27pm. Tim, forty miles away, stopped working and sat at his desk, doing nothing at all. He picked up his phone and stared at the blank display. It started to ring. He answered it and then listened, saying very little. Afterwards, he stood up and walked into his manager's office. His back was turned to everyone else but through the glass partition they saw his manager's face go white. A moment later he was leading Tim quickly back through the office. His hand, awkwardly, because he had never been a tactile person, was around Tim's shoulder. Something about his manner, and the expression on Tim's face – or the complete lack of expression – made everyone who was there stop what they were doing and watch. At the door hushed words were quickly exchanged and then Tim nodded and left. His colleagues were still staring when his manager returned to his office and put his head in his hands on the desk. He appeared to be crying.

PART 2

CHAPTER SIXTEEN

<hr>

Benjamin Tate had lived in the same flat for twenty years. It had two front doors. The first was hidden halfway down a small alley that ran between two houses and was invisible from the road. People had lived on that street for years, walked up and down it every morning and evening and never known of its existence. It was made of frosted glass and opened onto a flight of stairs that led up to a second door, a red one, wooden. The number four had lost a nail and slipped to an angle.

'Nice and quiet,' the estate agent had said, pushing it open with a flat hand that held the number in place until he was inside. 'You won't be disturbed here.' He was right in one sense of the word.

Now, after so long, Benjamin Tate knew it all so well, the spaces, the distances between the walls, the patches of floor that caught the sun – sometimes in summer, or on those bright winter days, he'd spend hours curled up on the carpet, following the warm yellow square as it moved gradually across the room. There were other times, particularly at weekends, when he would say something just to break the silence. Often then his own voice would startle him, sound alien, intrusive, like a disturbance. He'd feel the things around him cast a disdainful, reproving eye and turn away. Chastised, he would fall silent again and more hours would pass.

On this Tuesday morning he lingered in bed, taking pleasure in the softness of the mattress and the crisp, crack-and-whip feel of the sheets. Eventually he roused himself and slipped into the slippers and dressing gown that had been placed neatly on the stool the previous night. The kitchen was more a corridor, with cupboards leaning in from both sides and a small sink sulking at the end of it. The hot tap was stiff, had been stiff for years. It meant the water didn't come out at all and then suddenly it would gush, like a keeper of secrets finally letting go. Beside the sink the kettle had been filled to a finger's width above the minimum, and the coffee had already been scooped into the mug.

He took his drink into the living room. The buttons on the only chair stared cross-eyed at the opposite wall. He straightened one of its cushions and went to the window. Just on the other side of the glass the branches of an ancient tree were scratching to be let in. He liked the tree. He might have even called it his best friend. When he looked at it sometimes, he felt like it was looking back at him, especially on gloomy days, when its shadows and shapes turned into things other than themselves. He could see its eyes, dark knots regarding him silently from within a gnarled face. People spoke of the tree of wisdom, the sage, the sentient thing that watches through the ages. Over the years he'd seen it change and change back so many times, unveiling new versions of itself with the seasons, yet it was always the same thing. He respected that. A bird opened its wide wings. It flapped on its branch and then flashed black across the pale sky and was gone. Benjamin Tate sighed. He reached forward and fingered a date into the mist that had settled on the window, staring at it until it leaked over itself and disappeared. If only it could have really been like that. The big things had ended that day. He took pleasure in the small things now because the big things that had been planned for him, whatever they might have been, had ended.

Normally he would close his front door between 8.34am and 8.36am and that would afford him all the time he needed. There were mornings, strictly rationed, when he would adjust his schedule by twenty minutes. It was no small thing for Benjamin Tate, this breaking from routine, but when it was called for he would walk slowly to the café, slow enough to savour each of the 749 steps. This morning was such a morning. He had put on his black tie for the occasion. He owned a blue tie as well but the black tie was slimmer, more confident, a sartorial arch of the eyebrow, and in front of the mirror, at the third attempt, he'd got the length of it just so. Beneath the tie he wore the newest of his four blue shirts and a jacket that was also blue. Benjamin Tate had settled on his colours many years ago. In a rare moment of élan he had parted his hair the other way, and when he caught sight of himself in the Perspex of the bus stop he was, within his own limits, not cripplingly discouraged.

Although – and this nagged like a loose scab catching on his clothing – the brown shoes. He wondered what he'd been thinking. He had black ones. They had been sitting there waiting for him, right next to the brown pair, squared off, shining, ready for service. He'd even reached for them. But then what? It made no sense. Something had made his hand sweep past them and the next thing he knew his fingers and thumbs had clasped the heels of the brown ones and now here he was, halfway down the road already. He considered turning back. The colours didn't work together, they would undermine him.

But then he came upon the solution, genius in its simplicity, like a swimmer might come upon a warm patch in cold water; he need simply stand closer to the counter and she'd be none the wiser.

His pace quickened again. This, for Benjamin Tate, could be considered exuberance. He started humming. He decided Louis Armstrong was right, it was a wonderful world, and there were trees of green. He scanned the gardens for red roses. A cat appraised him from a low wall. Benjamin Tate squatted down and put his hand out. Is there any creature on this earth more capable of conveying contempt than the cat? He'd read somewhere that they spend much of their time plotting to overthrow their owners. Only size held them back. The cat noticed him with languid indifference, stood up, stretched out its lithe body and then settled back down, sphinx-like, looking the other way. With a derisive swish of its tail, Benjamin Tate was dismissed.

He continued on his way. He felt the morning on his cheeks, took covert delight in the sun and moon appearing together in the same clear sky; it was a bright new day and he resolved to be bright and new as well.

There was nothing special about the café. It was fitted out with three flimsy metal tables, one of which wobbled over a scrap of paper bent double beneath a leg. A chalkboard on the wall advertised full breakfasts, home-made lasagne and cottage pie, while a heater in name only cowered in the far corner. A draught blew whatever warmth it produced back in on itself. Benjamin Tate pushed open the door and his brown shoes propelled him forward into the room. *Deliberately casual* is perhaps the phrase; lips pursed as if he was whistling, but he wasn't; eyebrows knotted as if he was preoccupied, but he wasn't; a hand nonchalantly in his pocket, but that hand was clammy.

He gazed up at the day's menu on the opposite wall. It never changed. Near the window two women were slopping up runny eggs and spearing bits of sausage. A blue-collar worker sat at the broken table. Whatever had been there before him was seeping into his newspaper. The third table was empty.

Finally, Benjamin Tate allowed himself a glance towards the counter. Clare was looking directly at him. She smiled a hello and instantly he looked away. He started to rummage in his pocket for something he knew wasn't there. He looked at the two women who were both talking now. He looked back up at the menu that never changed.

Three boys burst in behind him. They were loud and immediately they filled the room with their loudness. They brushed past him and strode towards the counter. They didn't acknowledge Clare directly. Instead, in their loud, breaking voices they told each other what they wanted and how they wanted it and then continued talking amongst themselves while they waited for it to arrive. Then they were gone and Benjamin Tate was again standing alone on the sticky floor of the café.

Clare's hair on this Tuesday morning was dark red. It hadn't always been red. It had been black, blue-black, deep purple, sandy brown. It was down to her shoulders and that day she had tied it up in a high ponytail that exposed her ears and neck. There were wisps hanging lightly against her skin.

'Sorry,' she said to him, rolling her eyes. 'Boys will be boys.'

He began walking towards the counter. 'Yes, the boys,' he replied, pointlessly.

She laughed. 'So, what can I get you? Coffee, isn't it?'

'Yes. Thanks.'

And that's all it was. His special treat. Her fingertips

stopped short of touching his palm when she gave him his change – or perhaps he dropped his hand a notch to avoid contact – and then he was heading briskly out the door. He walked a short distance until he knew he was out of sight and then leaned against a wall. He looked at the polystyrene cup. He wasn't even thirsty. He thought of the date on the glass and sighed deeply, realising how tired he felt. He wondered if everyone found it such hard work being themselves or if it was just hard work being Benjamin Tate.

He looked at his watch. It was 8.37am. He brushed his hair back the other way and started walking again. He didn't want to be late.

CHAPTER SEVENTEEN

Benjamin Tate had worked at the same place for twenty years. It was a vast white building that dominated its block. Beneath it a basement had been hollowed out and buried within that basement were the medical records, a rolling history of health and ill-health, of everybody who'd lived, and was still living, in the district. The notes had been kept, meticulously, mercilessly, by the doctors who practised in the offices upstairs. Some worked there still, some had moved away, many were themselves now names on a card.

They'd been filed alphabetically, these loose, faded-by-time cards, in cumbersome metal filing cabinets with sliding drawers that clanged and clattered along their rollers. Years of heavy-handedness had bent many of their rails out of shape. Not all the drawers closed fully now; some, more than some, twisted in at odd angles and wedged inches short of flush. The cabinets themselves were stacked three and four high in long unstable rows that towered to the ceiling and barricaded the windows.

Benjamin Tate's task, and it had been his task for twenty years, was to collect these cards and turn the scribbles of blue and red and black ink into clear, chronological data entries. He ferreted along the dim alleyways, banging his shins on the sharp edges lurking in the shadows. He didn't stop to consider how many cards he'd processed, or how many still remained. Too many. And with every birth, one more still. He could remember his first. Carmichael. Dementia. And something else. Angina. Seventy-six years old. A widower. Since then he had learned all about human frailty. He had transcribed every malady and misfortune that can strike at the human body and mind. He had not missed a day. The three desks that sat alongside his, tucked into a tight alcove and weakly lit from above by one of those half-hearted, energy-saving lightbulbs, had been at various times occupied and unoccupied. The men and women who were there on his first day had long since drifted away. Their replacements too had been replaced many times over. Benjamin Tate, though, he'd survived – was that the word? It probably was.

On this Tuesday morning Benjamin Tate arrived at work at 8.56am. His brown shoes echoed in the stairwell as he descended. At 8.58am he sat down at his desk. He was the first to arrive. He switched on his monitor and while it whirred into life he checked to make sure all the items on his desk were still squarely aligned. When he was satisfied he picked up the batch of cards that had been correctly placed at a right angle to the keyboard the previous evening. Douglas, K. Obesity. High blood pressure. Diabetes. Douglas was forty-three. Carmichael to Douglas. Twenty years of life. He began tapping at the keys.

Over time his day had been divided into four subsections. From 9 to 11am was the first of them and it was all about finding a steady pace. He'd been a runner once and understood about rhythm and not going out too hard, too early. So, the first few hours were key to establishing an easy forward momentum, keeping something in reserve to make sure his race wasn't run by mid-afternoon.

It would be tempting, once he'd found his stride, to put in a bit of a spurt before lunchtime, to hit 11am and begin a gradual wind-up. But session two required discipline, keeping the brakes on. There's always a sense that the faster you work the quicker you finish, but he'd learned, down there in the basement, doing what he did, that work was a continuous thing. One card, ten or one hundred, the end would always remain out of sight, round one more bend. And he'd seen it before many times, those fresh faces, new blood that had trickled down through the floorboards to puddle up in the basement beside Benjamin Tate, ticking along at the beginning, all buzz and bluster, but then winding down like an old clock as the scale of the task dawned on them. 'How long did you say you'd been here? How long?' They'd stare at him in wonder, and that would be the moment, a stark, terrifying vision of the destination awaiting them. Many would be gone within the week.

So, Benjamin Tate was in no rush. One o'clock would come and go, the afternoon would start and session three, the dead time between 2pm and 4pm, when he was a long way from both the start and finish, would take its course. If he were to have a weak moment during the day it would occur here, when his powers of endurance might be examined. It was sometimes as simple as a lull, as though a parachute had suddenly opened behind him and was slowing everything down, but sometimes it was more than that, more like a strained tension, probably only fatigue-induced, but it had a physical quality and they would all feel it, like someone with a nasty past they all knew about had entered the room and was loitering just behind them. It would though, it always did, dissipate as 5pm approached and Benjamin Tate might permit himself a downhill run to the line, letting his step quicken and his hands tap at the keyboard with a touch more zing.

But this Tuesday morning was different, as he expected it to be, and by 9.16am Benjamin Tate was still holding the same card he'd picked up when he'd first sat down. He read it again. Douglas. Obesity. High blood pressure. Diabetes. Forty-three. Older than he was. There were dates down the side. If he turned the card over he'd know if Douglas was dead or alive. Two of the three other desks had been filled by now. He'd not noticed it happen. Where had these people come from, these fellow moles, not just the two that sat beside him now, but the dozens that, at one time or another, had sat beside him? Some had been older than him, many had been much younger. How and why had they ended up there? What could have happened to send them scurrying out of the light? Perhaps they too had... He stopped the thought before it developed. Obesity. High blood pressure. There was a barely legible note about exercise and diet. Benjamin Tate could just make out the word *yeast*. He looked back at the screen and then rubbed his eyes and started at the top again. Diabetes. 9.36am. Suddenly Benjamin Tate tore a strip off part of the card and stuck it over the date that had been glaring at him from the corner of the screen.

'Everything okay there, buddy?' Pete asked. Pete sat at the desk beside his. 'It's too early to be clock-watching, you know. And anyway, you've still got that bastard up there.'

He pointed up at the clock on the wall, then got up and disappeared behind the filing cabinets. When he returned he was carrying a stepladder under his arm. He climbed up and took the clock down. 'How's that, buddy? Better?'

Pete smiled again. He didn't belong there, in that basement. He looked like someone who should own a yacht, or have friends who did. He always said the right thing, and when he said the wrong thing he said it the right way, which seemed to matter more. But what Benjamin Tate liked most about him was that he treated everyone the same way, even the stranger types. He suspected it was less to do with goodness and more to do with self-absorption, a narcissistic bubble that enveloped him and enabled him, without difficulty, to remain unchanged, exactly who he was, regardless of his environment, but he didn't mind that. That made no difference to Benjamin Tate. He had once seen a painting of an ancient ship being tossed about on a wild sea. The scene was so visceral he could almost hear the damp wood creaking and groaning in the storm. Where had he seen it, that picture? Somewhere dark and dingy like this. But that's what Pete was like. What did it matter if the painter had witnessed the scene or imagined it, the effect was the same. Pete was still holding the clock in his hands, regarding it carefully. A flicker of something came to his face and he looked up at Benjamin Tate, grinning.

'Hey, you want to see time really fly?'

Suddenly he threw the clock like a Frisbee over the top of the filing cabinets. Three pairs of eyes watched it sail disc-like through the air. It seemed to hang forever, almost not moving, until it dived down and there was a loud shattering noise on the other side of the room.

'For Pete's sake,' he said, smiling at the now familiar joke. 'The old ones are the best. That's why I like you, buddy.' He winked. 'It's all good.'

Benjamin Tate was stunned. A little disturbed. He couldn't grasp chaotic gestures like that. It was too cavalier, too devil-may-care for his liking. There were rules, rules kept order, order was important. He watched Pete stroll back to his desk. Was it nonchalance? Nerve? Cocksureness? Probably a bit of all three, and other things besides. He didn't so much strut as roll sinuously in his joints. He had a way about him, did Pete. He turned over a card and moved his hands to the keyboard as if nothing had happened.

Benjamin Tate waited for whatever had been pitched sideways in his chest – that ship? – to right itself and then looked back down at his card. Douglas. Obesity. High blood pressure. Diabetes. Forty-three. Still alive. Living just three streets away. Married. Second marriage. Yeast-free diet recommended. He glanced at the screen and saw the bit of paper. It allowed him to go on.

Douglass, M. Dead. Dead for years. Aged fifty-seven. Stroke. A smoker. Benjamin Tate had never paused to wonder why it was necessary to store for posterity such records, records of the old, disappeared souls that no longer filled the gaps they once did. *Tap, tap, tap.*

Downes, T. Seventy-two. Arthritis in both hands. Mild depression. Cataracts. Chicken pox as a child. A long list. Benjamin Tate recorded it all.

Downes, V. Six. Measles. A bump on the head from a fall at school.

Dove, B. Ninety-eight. Ninety-eight and counting. Three cards' worth. All full on both sides. A scribbled story of survival. *Tap, tap, tap.*

Dover, B. Nineteen. Suicide.

Dovesett, K. Thirty-six. Appendicitis. Benjamin Tate checked both sides of the card but that was all there was. Appendicitis. Nothing more.

Dow, A. Sixty-two. Cancer. There was always one. No, there was always many more than one. He typed the word out and then read it silently in his head. *Cancer.* What was it about that disease that separated it from all the others, that stirred such feelings of disquiet and inevitability? It was the stalker you can't shake off. That's how it felt, as though it had singled you out even before you knew it existed and had, ever since, been closing grimly in. Is it really true that the Komodo dragon poisons its victims with a single bite and then patiently tracks the doomed beast down to the place where the toxins have finally felled it? The poor creature, what a way to go, shivering woozily beneath a bush in the sand, already on the brink, noticing, at a stage when it's too weak to do anything about it, those dead reptilian eyes staring lewdly at it from the other side of the clearing. Would there be a moment's pause, a moment of sizing up, one side assessing and the other accepting, or would that giant, low-hung head, all scales and hissing tongue, just keep swinging on the end of its thick neck as it advanced?

Doway, D. Sixty-eight. Cancer. Again. But in remission. Hopeful. The period after the bite, thinking you've escaped.

Dowdall, L. Forty-one. Stress. Asthma. Eczema.

Dowley... Downer... Downes... *tap, tap, tap*. Downing... Dowton... Doyley.

The steady rhythm. That easy pace. There was a cushion at his back and one on his seat. His mug had a picture of a palm tree wrapped around it. He'd never been anywhere where palms grew. That didn't matter. Its colours were bright against the background. The tape and card covered the date. The big things had ended. That didn't matter either. He'd have fish later. He always had fish on Tuesdays. The choice of fish, and how he cooked it, was variable. He was leaning towards hake. Possibly grilled. He didn't need to decide yet. The small things. The safety of the small things. A hand on his shoulder made him jump.

'Time to come up for air, buddy.' Pete half turned away but then stopped. 'You okay? You're as white as a baby's arse.' Benjamin Tate's breathing was fast. He put his hand to his forehead and noticed he was sweating.

'I'm okay.'

'You work too hard, buddy. Slow down. Come on, it's time

for our elevenses.' Benjamin Tate looked up at the clock. It wasn't there. Pete laughed. 'Long gone, mate.'

Benjamin Tate spent his lunch hours, when the weather was neither too much one thing nor the other, on the bench in front of the building. He would always try to be the last to get up from his desk, that way he could avoid the awkwardness of his colleagues passing by in one joshing mass and not inviting him to join them. Of course, it wasn't always bonhomie and pleasantries among the others. They, whoever they were that were occupying the desks alongside his, hadn't always got on. There had been splits, divisions, bullying, fallings out and makings up. Even the odd romance had blossomed, wilted, flowered anew. But these social comings and goings had always occurred apart from Benjamin Tate, near to him, but wholly detached from him. The current occupiers – Pete and Sophia and, what was his name? Darren? Dylan? – were friends. He had the impression that they knew each other outside of work, and had done for a long time. Certainly, Pete and Damien – Damien, that was it – were long-time friends. As for Sophia, well, a rose between thorns and so forth.

On this Tuesday, he exited the vast white building after them and took his seat on the empty bench. It was March 3. It was early spring but winter's fingertips still touched his neck and he pulled his collar up and ate his ham sandwiches under the thin sky and waited – he spent his life waiting, without ever wanting anything to arrive – for the hour to pass.

The day so far had been less brutal than he'd imagined. It was an anniversary, after all, an anniversary of sorts. But twenty years is an awfully long time. There were days now, even weeks, when he wasn't haunted. March 3 was never going to be one of them, and he didn't expect it to be, didn't want it to be. He never wanted to forget that he was responsible – he still called it *guilty* some days – for the thing that had happened. At the back of his mind he always wondered if he'd know her card before even reading the name, if he'd pick it up perchance one cold autumn day, with the wind buffeting the unseen windows, and some intuitive part inside of him would instinctively know it. He supposed then, and only then, he'd at last be able to climb out of that hole and never return. In the meantime, all those names, all those dates down the side continuing and continuing and then not continuing.

At 2pm Benjamin Tate returned to his desk. There was conversation left over from lunch that he was not a part of. Drakely. Draper... Many Drapers. Dredge.

Just before 4pm, when his hands were trembling too much to continue, he got up and went into the bathroom. He locked the cubicle door and wedged them between his thighs. He was not alarmed. He'd experienced something similar on many occasions. It was just a matter of waiting again; this time waiting for something to pass. The bathroom door opened and he heard footsteps crossing the tiles. He raised his feet above the gap beneath the door. He heard a tap turn on and then someone coughed and spat. Then silence. His hands were still shaking, more violently now, sending convulsions up into his arms. He clamped his legs tighter around them, used his shoulders to wipe eyes that wouldn't stop running. A second man entered. Benjamin Tate heard them chatting. He wondered how people could always think of something to say. Words begetting words. Then laughter. A tap again. More footsteps and then the bathroom was silent apart from a drip, curiously loud, echoing, like in a film. Benjamin Tate listened to it for a few more minutes and then, when he was sure he was alone, when he was sure the thing he was waiting to pass had passed, he unlocked the door and returned to his desk. By 4.59pm he was on Driffield.

So, hake. He heated the olive oil in the frying pan and then added the seasoned hake fillets, skin-side down. When the skin was beginning to crisp he added a few slices of butter to the pan, around the hake. He'd forgotten this step the first time, all those years ago, and had scraped and scratched at the pan until his meal was a scrambled mess. He didn't like mess. When he was satisfied it was just so, he turned off the oven and arranged two immaculately presented fillets on his plate, alongside a ladleful of peas. He ate his dinner quietly at the table in front of the window and when he finished he washed and dried the cutlery and everything else he'd used and returned them to their rightful nooks and crannies. He refilled the kettle to a finger's width above minimum and scooped a spoonful of coffee into a clean mug.

In the living room he turned on the television and stood motionless, gazing at it for a few minutes before turning it off and padding back down the hallway into his bedroom. He placed his slippers and dressing gown neatly on the stool and then climbed into bed. The softness of the mattress, the crack-and-whip feel of the sheets. He turned off the light and then looked up into the complete blackness of his room, waiting, again, for the day, March 3, to come to an end.

CHAPTER EIGHTEEN

Benjamin Tate rose at 5am, as he always did on Saturdays, and took off his pyjamas. Once they had been folded correctly along the seams and placed under his pillow he walked down the hallway to the airing cupboard. It was cold in his flat and without any clothes on his body shivered in the half-light. He stretched his stiff leg behind him and reached down to take out the polish, the disinfectant and three separate cloths – each had their role – and then hurried back into his room.

It always began there now. In the past when he'd noticed mess he'd addressed it immediately before moving randomly around the flat in search of the next task. What must he have missed? What horrors must have lurked in corners, behind doors, at the back of drawers? No longer. He knew better now. Now the exacting, exhaustive routine – back to front, side to side, a forensic sweep of every surface exposed to impurity – was long-established. There should be absolutely nothing arbitrary, he believed, about the cleansing process.

It was, mostly, a case of going over old ground. He could count on a single hand the number of occasions when someone other than himself had been in his flat. He didn't mind that.

Mysophobia is a fear of germs and contamination. Both were carried by other human beings. Alone, cordoned off from the world, he had turned his small space into a sterilised quarantine. He cleaned up after himself immediately. He put things he used back in their rightful place immediately. He disturbed as little as he could and as infrequently as he could, and anything that somehow slipped through – an insurgent crumb, a fleck of this or a spill of that – was unfailingly collected, corrected, during these weekly purges.

The bedroom was simple. There was hardly anything in it. He himself was hardly in it. In under an hour he had polished the windowsill, the bed-knobs, the supporting frames of the small chair. He had scrubbed the skirting boards and taken a toothbrush to the dirt that had gathered in its tiny cracks. The clothes from each drawer had been removed and, after the drawers themselves had been wiped clean, refolded and replaced. The same thoroughness, the same taking out and putting back, had also been applied to the wardrobe and to the bedside table.

It was still dark when he moved towards the bathroom. If there was to be a serious issue it would be here. He hesitated in the doorway, maybe he could just leave it, but something in his tummy stirred, sat up, sniffed the air, and Benjamin Tate was compelled forwards. Once inside he began a careful scan all around him, seeking out the areas of concern. As he turned he caught sight of himself, his trunk, in the mirror. He gasped. He was always surprised when confronted with the bloated creature that had swallowed him. He was looking at a shapeless mass of white flesh. Four graceless slabs hung from it. Everything seemed to be slipping off its scaffolding. He had run once. He had harboured great, ambitious dreams. And now this. He was taxed by the stairs leading up to his red door. He used hands to lift heavy legs up them.

Benjamin Tate looked away. There was dust on the bulb. That would mean there was dust on all the bulbs. Had he checked the bulb in his bedroom? And on the light on the bedside table? There was dust on the switch too, and on the wall socket. There was grime on the window. Perhaps it wasn't grime. Perhaps it was a trick of light and shadow. It could well be, at this time of the morning. Oh, if only he could have believed that. The tyrant that lived in his tummy would never abide such inattention, neglect even. He moved closer to the glass. It wasn't grime. It was a brown smear of something he couldn't identify. He backed away dubiously. The tyrant jumped to his feet. He was glaring. He was growing restless, agitated. Any moment now. When had he arrived, that sinister little cur down there, how had he seized such power?

'Okay,' Benjamin Tate said wearily. 'Okay then.'

Twenty years ago the clock in his room was an hour slow six months out of every year, more things hadn't been put away than had, letters, screwed up into balls and thrown under desks, would remain undisturbed for weeks. He envied that person, tried to remember what it was like to be him. He imagined it must have been like singing when you can't hear yourself.

Once the window was clean he got down on his hands and knees. He found the hardened slick of toothpaste at the bottom of the sink, spied the single hair in the crack between the tiles that demanded he clean all the tiles, scrape all the cracks. He was sweating despite his nakedness. Drops fell off his brow onto the cold floor that required more disinfectant, more scrubbing. The muscles in his arms ached. His fingers were about to cramp. Every so often he paused, sat up on his haunches and stretched out his spine. It was ever thus, one thing leading to another to another. There was the bathtub. He would scrub it. There was the toilet seat. He would wipe it. There was the bin, the shower handle, the inside of the taps. The kitchen would take hours. He pictured the oven, the fridge, the bacteria that would be permeating within both. He would vacuum all the rugs and the radiators and take the nozzle to the wiry carpet in the living room for maximum effect. It wouldn't be enough though. Why had no one invented a product that did the job as it was supposed to? People just played at cleanliness. No, he would have to get down there in the muck himself. He would have to press his cheek flat to the ground and pick away at all those things, real and not real, that were left behind, clinging on.

At one point in the late morning he gave up. He dropped the rag and the polish on the floor and then collapsed after them, rolling onto his back and letting his arms flop out next to him.

'There's nothing here,' he said. 'I'm done. Leave me alone now.'

Above him a fine thread of dust floated against the ceiling. From his prone position he counted four others in that room alone. He closed his eyes. The tyrant was up on his feet again. He was ranting. He was shaking his fist. He would never be laid down.

It was mid-afternoon when Benjamin Tate finally sat down at the small table. His lunch consisted of two fried eggs on a single slice of toast, as it always did on Saturdays. He ate slowly, cutting out small squares and chewing each mouthful thoroughly until it was like swallowing paste. He imagined it sliding down his throat and landing on the horrible little tyrant, burying him.

He knew where he came from of course, and when he had arrived. He'd been on the bus with him that day, about a year after the thing that had happened. Perhaps he'd been sitting behind him. Perhaps it had been his voice that had told Benjamin Tate to look at the old woman next to him, to notice the slick of saliva that had seeped from her mouth and was fermenting in a fold of her skin. She'd shown her gums to him then, and Benjamin Tate had nodded quickly and looked down. Her skin was sagging towards skeletal hands. On one was a plaster coloured with discharge. He looked away and the voice told him to notice the grease from a thousand heads on the window. Someone nearby had a wet cough. It dislodged phlegm and the voice said to him, *'They'll swallow that now.'* He started to listen to every cough and sneeze. *'How many cover their mouths, do you think?'* the voice asked. He imagined all the tiny particles of spit spraying into the air, all those invisible microbes circulating through the bus. They would settle on his cheeks and lips and in his ears and the corners of his eyes. He looked again at the old lady. She was staring straight ahead with flaps of skin dangling under her chin. She was wheezing. Her gaunt body was struggling to perform its functions. *'She's rotting,'* the voice whispered. *'That's rot coming out of her nostrils when she exhales. It's air that has been rolling around deep within her, through her veins, over her discoloured flesh, rubbing against and collecting all the decaying gunge that has gathered in the pit of her lungs.'*

He thought of the filthy air leaking out of everyone else too, spilling out of one mouth, sucked into another. He tried not to breathe. The bus jolted and he bumped into the window. There was a smear where his head had scraped against it. *'That's all in your hair now,'* the voice said. He looked at the old lady again. The drool on her chin was gone. He realised that was on him too.

Benjamin Tate pushed his plate away and sat back in his chair. Through the branches of the big tree he could see the market stalls on the high street. He looked at his watch. It was

2.57pm. The crowds were thinning. Some stalls were being folded away. No matter. He would wander down there shortly. He liked being absorbed into something larger than himself, to be, even briefly, one reed among many reeds swaying on the riverbank. What was it that Pete had said? 'There's two kinds of people in the world; Benjamin Tate, and everyone who's not Benjamin Tate.' He could remember the friendly squeeze on his shoulder and the way Pete had looked at him, not unkindly, as he sat back down. He'd not meant it to be as true as it was.

Perhaps he would see Clare there again, too, as he had done once before. He remembered the relief he felt, the preposterous relief, when he noticed that her friends were all female. Poor Clare. What would she think of him if she knew? He took his plate into the kitchen and washed it up. In the hall he swung his arms into his jacket and then squatted down to decide on his shoes. He was leaning towards the brown pair.

Suddenly he heard a noise. It was close, unnatural, it didn't belong there. He stood up and listened. After a moment it happened again, and he looked at the offending red door. He didn't believe it. It had done this to him before, knocked against its hinges, called him over and then sniggered behind his back as he stared at the empty square of carpet on top of the landing and the bare wall opposite. He waited. When the sound came for a third time he approached cautiously, and then, almost without warning, an arm wearing his coat was swinging up from his peripheral vision to open it.

CHAPTER NINETEEN

lare walked down the same road for the third time that afternoon. In her bag was a wallet. It wasn't hers. Finally, she spotted an alley tucked away between two houses and partially concealed by the trunk of a giant elm. Halfway down the alley was a glass door. She tried the handle. It was unlocked and opened onto a small stairwell that led up into shadow. She imagined ghosts and ghouls lurking up there among the cobwebs. As she climbed she became aware of a sharp smell. It became more pungent the higher she went and made her want to sneeze. On the landing was a second door, a red one. She tipped her head sideways to read the toppled over number four that was nailed to it, and then knocked.

The wallet in her bag had been handed in by a customer. At the close of day she had gone through it with a colleague to identify its owner and found his face – how old was he, thirty? Sixty? – staring out from a photograph on a card. She remembered him. He had been there a few days earlier, and many times before that. He never stayed long. He walked with a limp which was more pronounced some days than others, and he seemed always in such a rush, as though important things would remain undone until he and he alone had done them. 'But you must recognise him,' she'd said to her colleague.

'Oh, Clare,' her friend had replied, 'you're such a Florence Nightingale. Please be careful.'

She knocked a second time on the red door and then listened to the lack of noise on the other side. She looked at her watch. The market would be winding down now, the fruit left behind would be rotting in their crates. She looked for a letter box through which she could post the wallet. There was none. Perhaps she had missed it coming in. She knocked a third time and was just about to turn away when the door opened. He poked his head around it suspiciously.

'Oh hello,' she began. She wasn't wearing her work blouse. How unrecognisable people appear when seen out of context; in our heads we limit their lives to the parts and places where we overlap and we can't compute when they appear unexpectedly somewhere else. 'I work at– ' The door slammed in her face. The unnecessary violence made the brassy number rattle with rage. She hesitated, unsure whether to knock again or leave. After a moment a crack of light appeared, reappeared, between door and doorway, and a wide eye stared at her through it.

'Benjamin?' she said. 'Benjamin Tate?'

Clare was Clare George. She was twenty-four. She was kind and had duly suffered because of it. The world doesn't like kind things, doesn't trust them. When she was a young girl she used to give her pocket money to her friends. Her parents had scolded her but she'd argued, quite logically, that it was her money and didn't they want her to do things with it that made her feel good? But they had been right. By the time she was ten those same friends had started demanding things from her, things she hadn't wanted to give away. It came to a head when her father gave her a wooden box he'd carved himself for her birthday. Inside it were sentimental keepsakes; teeth of hers that had fallen out, locks of hair, drawings they'd dutifully held on to. Her friends – they were no longer her friends by this time – told her to hand it over and when she refused they took it from her by force, tipping its contents out into a hedge and running away laughing. Clare shouted after them but they ignored her. She watched them throwing the box between them like a ball. They kept dropping it and dropping it and dropping it. In spite of this, or maybe because of it, she refused to change. She sought the good in people, especially those people in whom it was harder to find.

Benjamin Tate stood before her now teetering unsteadily on a single leg. The other was wrapped behind it. His hands were hidden deep within pockets, pulling his shoulders forward and his head down. It created the impression of someone who was concealing as much of themselves as they could. He was blushing furiously. Every part of skin that was visible above the collar of his coat was deep crimson, and sweat pockmarked his hairline. She watched without looking as one bead then another dislodged itself. It was fascinating how they fell at different speeds, slowing, pausing, rushing on again.

'I have something you want,' she said. She took his wallet out of her bag and held it up before her. He stared at it for so long that she began to doubt it was his, before he extricated a hand and pinched a corner of it between two precise, pincer-like fingers. Immediately that hand squirrelled back into its hide, out of sight.

'You're very lucky to see it again,' she said. 'I've taken the cash out obviously, as a reward, but everything else is still in there.' He didn't react, and she looked at him strangely. 'I'm kidding.' They stood a moment then, each waiting for the other to do something. A loud faraway crack suddenly burst into the room, disrupting the silence. Everything stiffened and then slowly relaxed again. Individual raindrops, heavy and sporadic, began to tap loudly on the glass. 'Anyway,' she said, when she could think of no reason to linger, 'I had better leave you to it.'

Immediately he turned and walked into the room. She noticed his limp again, how he dragged a foot that pointed outwards. At the window he stopped but didn't turn around. What was it that intrigued her about people like him? But what did that mean, people like him? She didn't know him. Unorthodox people then, awkward people, those who make those around them uncomfortable. When her friend had called her Florence Nightingale she'd waved a hand at her and insisted she was finished with all that, with broken pipes that leaked out all the water she could give them – where had that line come from? – she must have rehearsed it. There had been a succession of these listless, impotent men that her generation seemed to specialise in, and she was fed up.

Joe had been the most recent of them. He was twenty-eight. He lived at home. He had no job, or rather, he had a hundred jobs and finished none of them. She had been halfway through another pep talk when she stopped, stood up, and told him abruptly that she was leaving. A trace of fear had passed behind his eyes, a recognition then that he needed to act, but oh-so quickly he'd found his way back to victimhood, had scowled at her and said if she failed to understand him, even she, then the whole world would fail to understand him, and he'd never stood a chance anyway. What had she ever seen in him to be so hopeful? What had she seen in any of them? She had always made their excuses and always been so disappointed to discover that they had none.

It was raining fully now. The glass drummed with noise. Beyond it the bark of the old tree darkened as it wetted. Perhaps she wouldn't go to the market after all. *Benjamin Tate.* She said the name to herself in her head. She could picture her friend tutting, her father looking at her with his sad, not-again-Clare eyes. But people were too quick to judge. She couldn't fathom why everyone was made so uncomfortable by difference, by the misunderstood or the opaque. She had always believed, or tried to believe, that what separates us, what marks us out as individual, should not be mocked or concealed, but celebrated. 'You're an old soul,' her father said. She doubted it. She thought she was too optimistic to be old in any way at all.

He'd not yet moved and she looked away from him, around the room. It was ludicrous. It was hard to believe he actually lived there, or anyone did. There were three bookcases, each full without any noticeable gaps on the shelves, but besides that there was no sign of him. She looked at the single chair, the table, the hunchbacked television the likes of which she'd not seen in years. The walls were bare. The smell that she'd first detected on the stairwell – she realised now it was the smell of hospitals – overpowered whatever human smell there might have been.

'It's very tidy,' she said. It was the kindest thing she could think of. He turned then and she smiled at him. He looked away quickly and shuffled off to the bookcases to busy himself there. She thought, oddly, of a skittish coyote circling on the outskirts.

'You have an awful lot of them,' she said.

'Four hundred and thirty-nine.'

She realised it was the first time he'd spoken. How small his voice was. It was tinny and difficult to hear. It came from his mouth but conveyed nothing of him at all. It didn't fit somehow. She went and stood next to him and he visibly flinched, pulling himself closer together, trying to occupy an even smaller space.

Occasionally she took a book out, paged through it idly, replaced it. Once, when she put a book back he took it out again and replaced it somewhere else, near where she had slotted it in but not exactly there.

'Sorry,' she said.

She wanted to tell him to take off his coat. He was sweating profusely and his obvious discomfort was making her uncomfortable too. She thought she should probably leave. She didn't want to be cruel. But that was also the reason why she stayed. The book she was holding now was called *Jonathan Livingston Seagull*. She held it up to him and he nodded, yes, he'd read it. 'Apparently he lives within us all,' she read. 'That's exciting then.' On impulse she dropped the book in her bag. She knew he saw her do it, but he said nothing.

'Have you read them all?'

'No. Not all.' She was about to say that she didn't blame him, that life was too short to spend it with your head down, that she always preferred to be outward facing, when he added, 'Three hundred and sixty-eight. I've read three hundred and sixty-eight. That's about eighty-four per cent.'

She managed not to smile. 'How do you know that?'

More sweat then. 'Please, take off your coat.'

He coughed into his hand. He said, even quieter than before, that he kept a ledger.

'You know, Benjamin Tate, that doesn't surprise me.' She could so easily place him at the table, writing down each title in alternative coloured inks to make it more legible. She wondered if he wrote down the dates he started and finished reading each book, assumed he did, with identical gaps between each word. 'Do you make comments too?'

'Sometimes.'

'Just sometimes?'

'Sometimes I can't think of anything good to say.'

She did smile then, but warmly. She wanted, inexplicably, to hug him. 'Ah, but there's always something good to say. If you want to say something good, that is.'

At the door she stopped. She tapped her bag, was about to say she'd return his book soon. 'You come to see me, don't you, at the café? I mean, that's why you come to the café. To see me.' She wasn't sure when she realised this. Maybe only as she was saying it.

He didn't respond. He appeared not to be listening. He was staring instead at the new gap on the shelf. When eventually he managed to face her he revealed an expression so full of private things that she felt she should avert her gaze. It excited her. Oh yes, she thought, she'd be back.

CHAPTER TWENTY

He looks older every year. That was the first thing Beth thought when she saw Tim wobbling between the tables towards her. Of course, everyone does, but he looked so much more than just twelve months older. The ageing process, which for so long had strangely seemed to overlook him, had taken hold now and the rate of erosion shocked her. It was the contrast to how he had remained unchanged for so long that was startling and made her, each time after seeing him, hurry upstairs and pull faces in the mirror to be sure the same catastrophe wasn't befalling her. They saw each other only once a year now, always on the same day, and for a number of years she was made incredulous by how he appeared immune to the wearing qualities of time.

'It's because my life stopped when hers did,' he said with a look that was both sorrowful and proud.

But then, one year, perhaps five years ago, he had emerged behind the window of the restaurant and even from where she sat she had seen that the degradation – is that what it was? – had begun. She'd stared at him aghast and hadn't been completely able to come to terms with his stricken appearance by the time he sat down.

'I saw the look on your face,' he said. 'It's no good smiling now.'

She had said to her new husband, for she had remarried by then, that it was as though the steady accumulation of days and weeks and months had finally reached critical mass and all at once come crashing down on top of him, and he had been ravaged by the colossal collapse; he moved gingerly, as though his limbs were constantly bruised, and his skull, now totally devoid of hair, was dented and the lifeless grey skin stretching over it was stained with red blotches. Since that day, each time they met she braced herself for the worst but each time the worst was beyond what she could have imagined.

He teetered in front of her now and then lurched forward as though suddenly shoved in the small of his back by an invisible hand. He gripped the back of a chair to steady himself and then winced. No, not a wince; she realised he was smiling.

'Well,' he said, 'here we are again.' He released the chair and shuffled around it.

They had started coming here, and on this day, March 3, while still in the painful process of unknotting themselves from the final threads of their marriage – although they hadn't known then that's what they were doing – and had, out of habit, out of duty, they never fully understood, continued to do so after their divorce. Beth, in particular, questioned the wisdom of it. She thought it unhelpful, unhealthy even. 'Don't come then,' he'd said, but she always did.

From the street the restaurant appeared tiny inside, but it was even smaller than that. The ceiling hung low and the tables crowded together so the backs of the chairs touched. When Tim had finally managed to fold himself into his place opposite her their knees bumped briefly beneath the table and she sidled subtly back in her seat.

'You look well,' he said, 'life must be kind to you.' She didn't answer him, she was trying not to stare, and he rephrased it. 'Is life being kind to you?'

It was a trap, of course. She knew that by now. He had asked her something similar a few years ago and she had made the mistake of answering openly. Her eldest had measles, she'd told him, and he'd not missed a beat. 'Your eldest? But surely you mean your second eldest?' He'd looked at her triumphantly.

'Tim. Please—'

'This is why we meet, see? Otherwise you'd forget her completely.' She had slapped him hard across the face then and stormed out while he shouted after her, silencing the other tables, that 'at least measles won't kill you,' that 'you don't die from the measles anymore, Beth.'

'I asked if life is being kind to you?' he persisted.

'It's fine,' she said flatly. 'Surviving.' She winced at her choice of word and hurried on before he could react. 'And how are you? And please stop fidgeting. It makes me nervous.' She looked at his fingertips. 'Are you smoking again?'

He closed his hands into a fist. 'No. But maybe I should. If it speeds things along, I mean.'

She concentrated on not reacting. This is what these meetings had descended into now, an exercise in neutrality and restraint. Because it was always like this: *if I was a horse they'd shoot me; life's awful and then you die; no one else cares so why should I?* An endless stream of bleatings. How long was she meant to put up with it? She wondered if he was always this person or if he became it just for her, which she suspected, as though, even now, he was competing with her for their daughter's affection.

'And Natalie?' she asked. 'Are you still together?' He stared back blankly. 'It was Natalie, wasn't it?'

He blinked and then made an elaborate performance of remembering. 'Oh, yes. *Was*. Past tense is right.' That wince-cum-smile again.

Ten years ago she might have leant onto her elbows and said, '*Oh no, what happened?*' A few years before that she might have cared what he said in reply. But now – now, already, she wanted to leave. This would, she promised herself, as she always promised herself, be the last time. She looked away from him. A sky-emptying rain was falling on the window and she stared at two dry spots on the surface of the glass, inexplicable islands untouched by the deluge. Why could he not accept it and move on? Until then she would never be wholly free of him, of it. Maybe he needed to die too. He looked about ready. But no, he'd persist, out of stubbornness, out of spite. She watched the rainwater bulge against the invisible edges before washing them away with one great surge.

'Forgive me, Beth,' he said. She looked back at him. He was staring at his hands resting on the table. They were shaking. 'Forgive me,' he said again, not daring to look up. 'I know how I must seem, what a strain it must be for you. But–' He did look at her now, and she was disturbed to see his eyes full of tears. 'But I see her in you still. Sometimes I can hardly stand to look at you.'

Outside on the pavement they stood uncertainly beneath the shelter of a canopy considering the weather as if seeing rain for the first time. It bounced off the tarmac and splashed the toes of their shoes.

'What I want to know is,' he said, 'what we did to deserve

this.'

Her stomach constricted with irritation. Her children would be home from school soon. She wanted to be there when they arrived. 'We did nothing wrong. You seem to think we're being punished. We lived, that's all we did. We lived a normal life, and what happened to us is a normal thing. Maybe not that exact thing. But tragedy is normal. We haven't been singled out for special punishment.'

'That's easy for you to say. Look at you now. It's like none of it ever happened, like the three of us, together I mean, as a family, were never even here.'

She bit down to hold in her first response. 'That really is a dreadful thing to say to me. I'm not sure how you can even say it, even if you don't believe it and are just trying to hurt me. I miss her every day. But I focus on the good things now. When I think of Ruby,' – saying her name out loud always shocked her – 'I think of rock pools. I don't know why. I can't remember where we were, which beach, we must have been on holiday somewhere. But I know it was very warm. And the water had been in the sun all day and was warm too. You must have called us because I'm looking over my shoulder and can see her little wet footprints on the big boulder.' She glanced sideways at him and decided to take a chance. 'She had been with me and not you for once, maybe that's why I remember it.' The corner of his mouth twitched, but not enough to tell. 'All I'm saying is, think of the good. It's easier.'

He didn't answer. He couldn't tell her, could hardly tell himself, that he wished she'd never even lived, that three years and eight months could never contain enough joy to make up for what had come since then.

'I need to go,' she said, feeling her wrist absently where once she wore a watch. She turned a full circle and stood facing him again. 'Tim, you're not still stalking him, are you?'

CHAPTER TWENTY-ONE

Benjamin Tate hunched over the table as though protecting what was in front of him from prying eyes. Can you be alone yet observed? He felt you could. Occasionally he peeked shiftily over his shoulder at the television. Things moved behind its screen. It watched him more than he watched it. On the paper in front of him was a mishmash of calculations. He'd worked out that twenty years comprised 175,000 hours, give or take a few, or more than ten million minutes. He'd estimated that as he'd never missed a single day at work about 38,000 of those hours had been swallowed up in that dim basement, while he'd slept through a further 58,000. That left a balance of 79,000 hours, which equated to 3,291.6 days recurring. Recurring! Even the terminology poked fingers. But so much time. What had he done with it all? He had often heard those around him moan about how busy they were, how hectic and fast-paced their lives, they complained about having too little time and too many things to fit into it, a surplus of things, things left over. He couldn't comprehend that.

Of course, a certain percentage of those missing hours

would have been absorbed by the natural physiology of things. The human body demands some degree of upkeep; nails keep growing, teeth need cleaning and hair cutting, the digestive system never desists from its function of filling and flushing, filling and flushing. But even all that together, it would only have occupied a small percentage.

He put his pen down and gazed out the window. A flock of blackbirds, or were they crows, clustered along the ridge of a roof. Suddenly all but one of them swooped down the slope and disappeared. Benjamin Tate watched the single bird that was left behind. It hopped along the tiles to the edge and then bounced up and down on its twig legs. It opened its wings slowly, experimentally, then closed them again in defeat and crouched back down.

He contemplated it absently. He supposed that many of those unaccountable hours had been squandered doing nonsense like this, gazing dolefully out at things, pointless things, everyday things that paid him no heed. What did he know? He knew when tiles blew away in storms and when they were replaced. He knew when certain windows were given new curtains. He knew about the dog that had sashayed along the driveway to meet its owner every evening until one day it didn't appear. For a month or more the lonesome owner, lonesome in Benjamin Tate's eyes at least, had traipsed to the door alone. Then, miraculously the dog was back. Its hind had been shaven completely, as though it was naturally hairless and had slipped on a furry jumper against the cold, and it was missing a back leg. He knew who had stolen the bicycle left outside, when the skyline had filled with aerials and other such monstrosities, and when the man with the dog had slammed the door and sped away for the last time. It wasn't much of a return really, knowing these things, not for 79,000 hours of life. What might he have done instead? It took 10,000 hours to master a new skill, yet he'd not learned a musical instrument, had never picked up a paintbrush, didn't even know the rules of chess.

The flock of crows or blackbirds – or were they ravens, what was the difference, was there a difference, why had he never found out, with all that time on his hands? – had returned now, had settled around its flightless friend so it could no longer be told apart from them. That pleased Benjamin Tate, relieved him in some obscure way. He stood up and opened the window. He had a vague idea he might applaud. A thin branch that had been bowed against it twanged into the room. The movement scattered the flock for a second time and again he found himself watching the solitary bird that remained. Was it the same one?

'*Be brave.*' That's what he'd written in his ledger, alongside the entry for *Jonathan Livingston Seagull*. '*You can still fly high. There is still time.*' The letters, in blue ink, were all the same height and comfortably spaced. But he'd come back to it that day, or a later day, and in angry red writing that broke the lines he'd scratched: '*You don't deserve it!*'

He walked over to the bookcases. He tried to recall which ones Clare had touched and he touched them also. He stood where she had stood and inhaled the air she had exhaled, imagining the atoms she'd left fizzing in the room attaching themselves to him. In his bedroom he took off his clothes and put a hand on the soft bundle between his legs. He lifted it up, let it drop again. It made a flat, slapping sound. Skin on skin. He prodded it like a child might prod a lifeless hamster.

'Good heavens,' he said, 'the state of that.'

He'd been dead for years. He thought of his children, the ones he had never and would never father. Two boys, always two boys, but only one ever appeared properly to him. He had short, straight brown hair and long, girl-like eyelashes. The second son was never seen, was always just accepted as being there, as happens in dreams sometimes. They burst in on him at rare moments, bringing with them on their coats and in their hair the smell of the outdoors. Their shrieks and whoops would scatter the silence and for a short while everything would come alive. He'd stand in its midst and watch until the long-lashed one stopped suddenly and stared, as if surprised to see Benjamin Tate there. He would panic then, trying to think of what he might say to make them stay. But he never could, and whatever whirlwind had carried them in would carry them out again and, always, all at once, he would find himself gazing dully about him, with only the big tree and the books on their shelves for company while the silence crept stealthily back.

His boys, faint phantoms in the air of little people who had gone or not quite arrived. They never aged. Yes, he missed them terribly. There must be a place, or many places, where all the things that could have happened are happening still, where the longed-for things are being lived out.

And their mother, where was she? Who was she? He didn't need to wonder. She was Madeline of course, in these fantasies, or delusions rather. Had that really been her in the passing car, staring at him, mouth agape, however long it was now? He felt it must have been simply because of the impression it had made on him. One thing he'd never forgotten about her was how tightly she'd held his hand, not just the first night, but every night. He'd felt at the time, arrogantly – but aren't all young men arrogant? – that she gripped him like that because she'd been suspended above a great chasm and he was the only one holding on to her. He'd felt the weight of her pulling at him and eventually he had let go. He saw her falling and falling into the abyss until the blackness swallowed her up. He'd been wrong, of course. They'd been upside down, and the dark well had been beneath him the whole time.

All that life. All that life he had actively, deliberately deprived himself of. '*You don't deserve it,*' he had written. He looked again at the numb appendage dangling dormant between his legs.

Benjamin Tate opened a drawer now and retrieved the only pair of shorts he still owned – they came with a belt and zip – and a short-sleeved shirt that had a collar and buttons. They would have to do. He put them on and then, avoiding the mirror, looked at the slippers and the dressing gown sitting patiently on the stool. He shrugged at them. 'Everyone has to start somewhere,' he said. 'Or start again somewhere.'

The park was unchanged despite all the years. The tennis courts had gone, had been replaced now by a playground that didn't resemble any of the playgrounds he'd played in, while the old playground, the playground where he'd met her, was a ruined and desolate thing on the far side that nobody had bothered to dismantle. He wondered how long graffiti lasted.

He began shuffling along the path that ran around its perimeter. How many times had he been along this path? Once upon a time he'd been the Pope of the Park; that's what he had dubbed himself, from the puffs of white smoke that trailed after him when he ran on winter mornings. Now he felt like an imposter. He was the slogger now. He had known immediately that he'd never run again, after the thing that had happened, at least not the way he had. His right kneecap had split in two when the key had gone through it. Part of his patella had escaped to the back of his leg, out the way, while a much larger part had shot halfway up his thigh. Sitting in the car afterwards, his fingers had traced its shape beneath his skin, not realising what it was. But the real damage had been done to the wires and cables behind the knee, the bits that held all the other bits in place. That is what had brought about a permanent end to his days as an athlete.

He kicked his legs out a few times, trying to loosen them up, and then leant over his waist towards his toes. He'd been able to place his palms flat on the ground once, now he hung on the end of taut hamstrings with his hands no lower than the middle of his shins. His knee, lined with scars, was in front of his eyes.

He began walking, cautiously at first, then a little brisker. He broke into a slow jog. It felt odd. He remembered how his arms had relaxed at his sides and he tried to recreate that feeling, loosening his shoulders and letting his elbows bounce. *Tap. Tap. Tap.* He waited for his breath to find a rhythm in time with his step. It didn't feel like it should. He waited. Another runner passed him coming the other way and smiled.

Faintly, in the background, his knee began to throb. He passed the playground. There was the bench. What had possibly become of her? He realised he was waiting for her card to land on his desk too. Suddenly a searing pain shot up his leg and he lurched to a stop. He cupped his knee in both hands and breathed steadily.

He'd not kissed anyone since Madeline. He tried to remember which had been the final kiss. So often final times pass unnoticed while we're thinking of bigger, better things to come. There had been girls since her, but like Clare, they had never known it. The affairs had all played out in his head, had been no more than outlets for the hopes and hankerings inside him that had nowhere else to go. There was the blonde girl whom he'd first seen at the bus stop, and Becky, fulsome Becky, with the wicked laugh that suggested she was laughing at something other than the joke. And Louise, who ran a market stall selling hats, and Tanya, who cut his hair, and Tina, Tabatha, Tracy... These weren't their real names.

He had made a more decisive effort once, at what exactly he wasn't sure. It was a faltering, misguided effort, and it served only to reinforce his belief that this world was not meant for him, nor him it. He had gone to visit a lady whose advert he'd found in the local newspaper at a time when local newspapers still existed and such ladies still placed such adverts in them. She'd opened the door wearing an elaborate get-up that comprised mostly of string to which small, desultory triangles of pink material had been attached. It made him think of catapults. There were, in places, if he remembered correctly, tassels and fluffy borders. She'd asked for the money and then when he'd handed it to her, such a strange sensation, she'd turned her back on him and walked into her room. He could still see her small buttocks rubbing together, twisting the black string that was half buried between them. The room was dark. Curtains were drawn and there was a weak lamp on the floor. Something had been draped over it, a T-shirt perhaps, subduing its light still further. What was it that visitors were not meant to notice?

In the middle of the floor, almost occupying it completely, there was a bed, large and hollow and flimsy-looking. He wondered how it stood up to the treatment it must receive. Sprawled over the mattress was a scruffy white blanket that in later years, when his phobia was full-blown, he'd never have touched. She'd pointed to the bed and he'd sat down. A yard in front of him she began to unbind herself from the rigging that had been erected around her sparse frame and he turned his gaze to the gap between his feet. She glanced up. 'You.' She waved a finger in his direction. 'Take off.' He leant forward and began to undo his shoelaces. Her bare feet padded out the top of his vision and then a light switched on somewhere. He heard urine splash into a bowl and looked up to see her sitting on the toilet. She seemed then to remember he was there and reached over and swung the door closed. He heard the toilet flush as he scampered away.

He began tentatively to run again. He could feel his feet in their inappropriate footwear, the brown shoes, thudding into the ground. He was half limping. He knew it wasn't an economical motion, that it made his legs go out to the side and that anything not moving forwards or backwards was wasted energy. He'd said that once. Here, in this very park. The past makes a mockery of us all sooner or later. The pain was unbearable now and he stopped again. He bent and flexed and twisted, trying to release whatever had seized up.

He was sure Clare had inclined her head before leaving, the way people do sometimes who want to be kissed.

He looked at the next lamppost, calculated that it was no more than fifty yards away. He used to run when he was confused, he used to run when he was worried, when he was annoyed, elated, melancholy. He set off on a third, final attempt. The hot poker inside his leg twisted up into his hip. He kept running. The lamppost was forty, thirty-five, thirty yards away. He was not limping anymore. It was something else, something even more ungainly. The runner he'd seen earlier passed again. Benjamin Tate noticed the look on his face. Now twenty-five yards. Now twenty. He passed the playground where he met her, the bench where he left her. But it wasn't about her, had never been about her. His mind only snagged on her because it wasn't brave enough to confront what had come after.

What if he'd sat longer on that bench, even thirty seconds longer? He saw himself getting up. *Stay*. He saw himself getting in the car. *Stay*. He saw the car reversing out of the car park, speeding down the road, approaching the roundabout. He'd spent twenty years, 175,000 hours, shrinking his existence from that very moment into the smallest nothingness imaginable, striving for the lack of life that he'd that day visited upon her. Her. He couldn't even speak her name.

He collapsed to the ground. Crippling pain. He'd never considered its literal meaning. Such an apt turn of phrase.

CHAPTER TWENTY-TWO

'S talking,' she had said. '*You're not still stalking him.*' Such a sinister word. And so untrue. In Tim's mind you had to know where someone was to stalk them. He preferred to call it '*seeking*'.

He paced again up the road. He knew many of the people who lived there – knew them to look at, at least – but not all. It was the ones he didn't know that drew him back. He wondered how many recognised him through his different disguises. Some surely must. There was the twenty-something man with the shaven head and designer stubble. He wore V-neck T-shirts, mostly pastel coloured, that he'd either grown out of or had been too small to begin with. At the end of his lead was a dog that yapped rather than barked, that didn't reach his ankles, its tiny legs moving ten to the dozen along the pavement. His parents, or people Tim assumed were his parents, often left his house with a basket full of dirty laundry. There was the man and woman a few doors down. Her hair had been long and sumptuous when Tim first arrived, but then she'd cut it all off. Weeks later Tim realised he'd not seen the man again. Where were all the children? There must be children in these houses.

He never saw them though. He was grateful for their absence, they're so much more curious about the world around them.

'Working late?' asked Evel Knievel. Tim had labelled him thus because he would spend the long summer evenings on his drive, tinkering with his bike. Bent at its side he'd rev it endlessly, head turned and a faraway look in his eye, and then suddenly he'd stop and his spanner would again probe its insides for whatever grunt or growl had so offended him.

'No rest for the wicked.' Tim smiled. 'Another day, another dollar.' He marvelled at how badly he could play these parts without evoking suspicion. Today he was the Council Official, which meant white shirt, short-sleeved and slightly ill-fitting, specs either perched on his forehead or hanging in front of him and, inevitably, the clipboard and pencil. How many evils could one carry out unchallenged if one had a clipboard to blind prying eyes and bat away awkward questions before they were ever even formed?

He had other personas. The Postman, obviously, The Jogger – and sometimes he did still jog so this worked on multiple levels – The Traffic Warden (which he'd now abandoned), the Bored Man with the Traffic Cone, and the Common Man in Overalls. They were all effective, and so far removed from his actual job that he even took some enjoyment from it. He thought of his partners, his clients and prospective clients. If only they could see him now. Where had he been in the last six months? He ran through his itinerary: Rome, New York, Hong Kong, Dubai, Nairobi, Dublin, Athens, Madrid, Beijing – or was Beijing the previous year? Semantics. He had been there, that was the point. And now he was here, standing officiously beneath a lamppost on a nothing street in a nothing town, scanning the pavements with furtive sideways sweeps. Did he expect to find what he was searching for, what he was always searching for, when he came here? Of course not, not anymore, but he came regardless because it was the only valid form of expression of his crusade – that's what he called it now – when all else had failed. He shook his head at the mystery of it.

Simultaneously, he noted satisfactorily that the gesture emphasised his act, made him appear even more the befuddled administrator tackling a stubborn drainage issue or whatnot. In fact, what really perplexed him that early evening was how, in this technological age when everyone left a digital impression wherever they went, and even places they didn't go but only considered going, he'd still not managed to find him. How? How was that possible? He'd expected it to take ten minutes on his phone when, five years ago, he'd sprung off the sofa and said, 'I must find him. I must find him now.'

'What? Who?' A woman, not Natalie, had been beside him. He ignored her.

'And then I must kill him.' He was standing ramrod straight in the middle of room. 'I'm not sure about that. But I must definitely find him.'

He balanced the clipboard on the crook of one arm and with the other ran a hand softly along the handle of the hammer that hung inside his trouser leg. He pinched the metal head between his fingers, taking pleasure in its heavy, unyielding surface, and knocked his knuckles with quiet approval against the metal. He pictured this boy, but he'd be a man now, of course, turning the corner and walking straight towards him, oblivious of the ambush he was strolling into. What happened next never completely materialised in Tim's imaginings; being there, waiting with intent – that seemed enough to becalm him.

He'd not chosen this street at random. How foolish that would have been. No, he had chosen this particular street, at this particular time of day, because it was here and – he glanced at his watch – about now, that he'd seen him before. His back had been turned, but the limp had given him away. It was always the gait with them, wasn't it? Uncanny. Once his own clumsy shuffle had been the thing that singled him out, and now the roles were reversed. Such symmetry.

'It's you,' he'd said then. He'd looked around. 'It's him,' he'd said, but no one had paid him any attention. He'd even raised his hand and pointed. And then? And then nothing. He'd just stared, slack-jawed, as the limp went away from him. He'd spent countless nights since then wondering how the boy hadn't heard him, why he himself had just let him go. He doubted, sometimes, if it had ever even happened at all. But the assumption that it did compelled him back here. Not every night, not most nights, not even many nights, and entire months would pass sometimes, but then the urge would be back. It wouldn't return slowly, building up over a few days – a vague idea, a thought, a serious consideration – until it could no longer be ignored. Nothing like that. It would simply not be there and then be there again, as real and reasonable as the sun, as though it had been there all the time and he'd just this moment noticed it again. He never doubted it. He would leave work early. If he was overseas he would fly back from wherever he was. Nothing continued as before until he'd returned here.

It was dark now. He had the sense that he was starting to loiter. Even the clipboard didn't defend him indefinitely. One more pass, then that's it. He saw no one. He reached the end of the road and turned around a final time. A movement. A change in the light just over there. He leant forward, frozen. But it was nothing. Just a dog. He was relieved. He turned again and left, hoping he'd not be back again for a long, long time.

CHAPTER TWENTY-THREE

Clare was sitting cross-legged on the carpet. She was painting her nails. Occasionally she splayed her fingers and tipped the wings of her spread hand to catch the raft of light from the window. Benjamin Tate, watching from the chair, would be cast back then to long-ago days when he used to walk home from school, watching with one cocked eye down the length of his arm as his own hand dived and arced against the dark green of the hedge.

She had not spoken now for nearly ten minutes and he was beginning to think it, she, wasn't real. But his imagination didn't stretch this far, and he need only extend a leg to kick her knee. Absurd, that's what this situation was, impossible and completely absurd. Her cup was on the floor just over there, with lipstick on the rim. He had made her that cup half an hour ago.

'Sugar, milk?' he'd called from the kitchen, as though he was a normal human being and this was a normal part of his day. It was his wallet. That's how all this started. What angel had reached into his pocket that day? Perhaps despite all he'd done he still had a friend in a high place.

'I enjoyed it,' Clare had said when she'd first arrived.

She'd handed him the book and he'd walked as calmly to the shelf as he could and filled the gap that had been irking him for days. Each morning and evening he had deliberately not looked at the conspicuous wedge of shadow that should not have been there. He had tried to mask it, minimise it, by shuffling the other books along, but that had only created more gaps elsewhere. What was it about incongruous spaces, moulds in the air in the shape of the thing missing, that troubled him so much? He was never able to see what was without fixating on what wasn't.

'I've not been able to look at birds the same way since,' she'd continued. 'Although it's not really about birds, is it?'

He looked at the wall behind her, the doorframe above her, anywhere but directly at her. It was because of the dress, the dress and the way she'd done her hair in tight coils that he could imagine someone gently pulling just to watch them spring back into place. He assumed that she must be on her way out, or on her way home after being out. But she seemed in no rush at all. He had turned from the bookcase to find that she'd followed him into the room and after a few minutes hovering she had promptly sat down where she stood. He had hastened into the kitchen then to escape, and when he returned with the two cups she was still there. She had glanced up from her nails and nodded at the chair, his chair, and he sat. Her dress had ridden up her thighs a little. She was wearing black stockings. Almost immediately he felt himself begin to perspire.

'It made me think of my father,' she said. She was still talking about *Jonathan Livingston Seagull*. 'The flying parts of it. He's a pilot in the air force. Or he was. He's not allowed to fly anymore because of his eyes. I'm sad for him. He misses it. He says he doesn't, but he does. He's my best friend. What about your family?'

There had been a beastly storm overnight. The first leaves

of spring had all been shaken off and the bare branches shuddered in their new nakedness. Far above them small clouds scudded along at great pace. From his seat he couldn't see, but had seen many times, the weak shadows that would be trying gamely to keep up, slithering over one rooftop then another.

Yes, what about his family, what had become of them? It had been Charlie's birthday the previous week. He would have liked to have sent a card had he known where to send it. He looked back at Clare. She frowned at her fingernails, wiped away the polish and began again.

'It's like one long awkward silence,' she said, not looking up, 'coming here, I mean. Only it's not awkward. Despite you.' She did look at him then, peering up through long eyelashes. 'I'm confused though. How long did you say you'd lived here?'

'I've been here a while.'

'A while,' she repeated absently. She looked all around her, then back at him, and tilted her head as she was wont to do. 'So, I hope you don't mind me asking, but where is everything?'

There was the table, the small chair, there were the bookcases and the television that watched him as much as he watched it – why was that, why did he feel always that vague sense of being observed? Everything was right there.

'Everything is right here,' he said.

'No, but I mean–' She stopped, smiled the way someone smiles when they don't understand the joke. 'You should see my room.'

An image of her bed flashed across his thoughts. He began perspiring fully then. He felt the heat coming into his face and a single bead trickle from the pit of his arm and down his side beneath his shirt. The first thing he'd have changed about himself – maybe not the first thing, but a thing – was how he never stopped assessing his performance in life while it carried on around him.

'My room is overflowing with...' Clare searched for the word, 'clutter, I guess.' She told him then how they had moved all the time when she was growing up, how they had lived on exotic bases all over the world but never the same base for long. 'It was only what I brought with me that made it home. I couldn't bear to throw anything out.'

'I keep all my books,' he said.

'Yes, that's true. All four hundred and something of them.'

'Four hundred and thirty-nine.'

She contemplated that for a moment. 'It's not so different, really. The things I keep, they're stories too. Just my own stories.'

She was, somehow, more beautiful than she looked. He remembered what his mother had said about people being Christmas presents, that what they looked like was the wrapping paper and that the real gift was inside. To his horror Benjamin Tate began suddenly to weep. Large bulbous tears streamed silently out of his eyes without any good reason. He gathered the cups and hurried into the kitchen. When he returned she was standing by the door. She was holding his coat.

'Shall we go then?'

They were beside the canal now, walking in the watery sunlight. She wasn't holding his hand. He had thought perhaps she might. The path was narrow and unruly bushes kept impeding their progress, forcing them into single file. He realised he'd never seen her from behind. Her shoulders were broad, like a swimmer's, and her hips seemed to belong to a larger woman. How round and marvellous and opulent they were in that dress. He saw beneath it and beneath her skin to the skeleton, to the bones that rolled and rose one side then another, making everything sway. How old did she say she was? The people that came in the opposite direction, that looked from her to him and back to her again, they wondered what she was doing there. He wondered that also.

'We're so lucky to have places like this to come to,' she said. A heron stood on the far bank, long and slender, beak turned up to the sky, its reflection rippling beneath it. 'Quiet places. I know I talk a lot, but the truth is I prefer the silence.'

She stopped walking then and turned to face him. One of the coils of her hair was uncoiling in the damp dusk air and she brushed it out of her eyes.

'Can I ask you something, Benjamin?'

'Yes.'

'Has something happened to you?'

'What do you mean?'

'I don't know. It's just... I like to help people.'

He didn't answer. She walked on a little, slowed, waited for him to draw up alongside her, then they walked on together. Behind them the heron watched them depart through blank, black eyes. Eventually, satisfied, it launched itself off its low perch and swept past them, flying flat over the water with great, slow swoops before gradually climbing higher and higher on its wide wings.

'Here,' she said a little later. The town was far behind them now. 'Let's sit down. It's my favourite spot.'

Through a gap in the hedges the bank rose away sharply to a level patch that was sheltered from the wind. The ground was damp and he took off his jacket for them to sit on. From up there they looked down through the light that was flattening into a dullish blue-grey towards the path and the canal. He'd seen a fox in there once. It had been perfectly preserved in a sheet of ice, its lustrous coat was still a healthy chestnut brown and apart from the fact of it being dead it appeared completely untroubled by the ordeal. The water below stirred then stilled. Whatever had disturbed it had sunk back down into the grim depths. What must it be like down there, on the bottom, the things that must coming apart piece by flaky piece.

'I didn't mean to pry earlier,' she said.

'No, it's fine.'

'But if you ever want to talk about anything, anything at all… I don't judge people. Sometimes just saying something makes it go away.'

He wanted to kiss her; more than that, he wanted her to kiss him. He wasn't sure but he must have had a dream the previous night. He awoke from it to the shocking but not unpleasant surprise that his entire body, every inch of it, was awake. He had lifted up the duvet and opened his knees. Yes, it had been undeniable. He'd put his hand down there and held it for a moment. It was surprisingly hot and he'd been able to feel it pulsing.

'It's just that something is meant to happen,' Clare said, 'to us, or between us. Don't you feel it, too?'

A cyclist passed in front of them. Benjamin Tate followed him along the path until it turned his head and he found himself looking at Clare's fixed profile. She hadn't noticed the cyclist. He had simply passed through her line of sight, like a deer might pass through a sunbeam in a forest. As he watched, her lips parted ever so slightly, drawing out between them a silver, glistening thread of saliva. Suddenly she turned to face him. The directness of her action froze him and he felt his mouth instantly dry up. A section of his brain wondered about the way fluid moves around the body, why his tongue and lips were thick like cardboard yet his brow, his palms and his spine prickled with sweat. He could feel her breath, cool and a little stale in his nostrils.

Something is meant to happen between them, she'd said.

She must not know him. Nothing ever happened. But this was happening. *'Be brave'*, he'd written in that stupid ledger. He leant towards her.

'Oh,' she said, jumping up. 'Oh no. I'm so sorry. I– That's not what I meant.'

CHAPTER TWENTY-FOUR

'Please,' Clare said, 'wait, don't go. I'm sorry. It's my fault.' He was half walking, half falling down the bank. 'Benjamin, wait.' She said more after that but he was moving faster than her, despite his knee, and the breeze that blew along the canal carried her voice away. On the path, cosily hugging itself, a duck was asleep on its webbed feet. Its soft body, stout in the middle and tapering at the head and tail, was the same shape as a rugby ball balancing on its tee. He imagined his boot catching the bird flush, the choked squawk, the sudden rush of air and whatever else being expelled through the too narrow gap. He imagined the largest section of whatever would remain of it, the crushed middle part with its caved-in flanks, flying through the air and splashing flatly on the far side of the canal, like a carrier bag full of small stones.

Who was this Clare, really? Where had she come from? How quickly she'd bounced up onto her feet, as though fearing he might try to inflict another kiss on her. He wanted to scream at her. More than that, he wanted to take out this rage on himself. He didn't think he was a special case. He thought he was far less than that. He thought that on every street, perhaps in every house almost, there were people who had carried greater burdens, who had seen greater obstacles placed in front of them and had overcome them. He was a less than a special case. His obstacle was still there. For twenty years his nose had been pressed up against the sheer face of it. He wondered, truthfully, if he'd ever properly tried to get over it, or around it, or through it. Maybe he had. But what did trying look like? Maybe he'd tried so hard he'd smashed himself to pulp against it, that all he was now was a dark, liquid stain, absorbed into it, part of it.

He was walking, lurching rather, pitching forwards. His body was taking him home. There was that cat, on the wall again. It was the same cat as before. It arched its back and hissed and then jumped onto the pavement and loped away across the road in that soundless way that all cats have. He turned left. It wasn't late, but the streets were quiet. Dark pools swirled between the lampposts. Cars parked up against the kerb eyed him anxiously as he approached, braced as he drew level, relaxed as he passed. He felt, alongside the anger, a sort of liberating elation. A low branch hung down and he reached up, snapped it and dropped it over his shoulder without breaking stride. All around him the houses were closed up, doors closed, windows and curtains closed. Behind them the families would be settling in for the night, telling their stories. And his family? Those two little boys that played about his heels, his wicked and wild wife? Where were they? He thought of his empty flat – empty even when he was there – silent, unmoving, lifeless, devoid of life, unlived in. He wanted to be there again, right now, with a heavy implement in his hands. He saw himself tearing at things, pulling stuff over, breaking things, throwing them into harder things and then stamping on whatever of them remained. He slapped himself in the face so hard it made him yelp. There was relief in that. He did it again. Why had he never self-harmed? He imagined that had he started he might never have stopped.

He strode on. He wasn't going home. He had assumed he was but had already passed his flat. There was that white building, still white even in the dark, white in the reflected glow of the stars and the moon and all the other lights whose effervescence was somehow absorbed by it. It rose up from the ground, towered over everything like it believed itself to be some great monument to heroic deeds. He had wasted most of his life there. All his adult life. He wanted to take a torch to it. He would. He would, but not tonight. He circled around its perimeter and kept going. He knew now where he was going. It wasn't far. It had never been far, yet he'd managed, somehow, to never go back.

'My friend calls me Florence Nightingale,' she had said. 'I just like helping people, is that so terrible? Let me help you. Tell me why you are the way you are?'

'The way I am? I've managed for twenty years by myself,' he'd shot back. 'I don't require an intervention.'

'What happened twenty years ago?' she'd asked keenly.

He was approaching it from the other side now. Would it look the same? What, he suddenly wondered, if it was no longer there? Town planners were always busybodies, looking for new ways to justify their positions. But no, it would be there, unchanged. He knew it would. It was no distance now. Less than a mile. He was walking as fast as he could. If only he could have run.

Maybe he should have just grabbed her, Clare that is, or Madeline, or that old whore, or anyone. What did it matter? That feeble, trembling little creature he'd hid inside for so long, he wanted to grab him too, shake him, shake him until he dropped down dead. He wanted to drag what was left to a bridge and dump the limp weight over the edge. He imagined the slow submerging before the black surface closed over where he'd been. He heard, shockingly through the silence, a horrible shriek. He realised the noise was coming from himself. All around dogs started barking. He hurried on. To his left was a supermarket, unnaturally bright on the far side of the deserted car park. Where was everyone? What time was it, really? He kept going, past the bus shelter, also empty. His knee was aching now. *Good, let it ache.* He approached a bin pinned to a pole and drove his knee into its side with all the force he had. Maybe that's why the cars had winced. He collapsed on the ground and remained there for several minutes. Eventually he pulled himself up using the pole and walked on.

And then, all at once, he was there. He stood on the bend and looked down at the soft grey of the pavement's ridge and the gutter, the black tarmac in front of him, the roundabout a short distance away. He looked to his left and saw a concrete wall – that was new, or different – behind which he saw the top of a brick building which he knew was the electric substation.

He stepped off the pavement and walked a few paces. He looked both ways down the road, then down at his feet. He couldn't be certain, but he imagined he was in the exact spot. He stood very quietly and paid close attention to his body, searching out new sensations, listening for the beginnings of things profound. He expected to feel something, although he wasn't sure what, but he felt nothing. He sat down and waited.

'You want to get off there,' a voice said. On the opposite side of the road an old man had stopped walking and was watching him. He had both hands on his hips. One hand had been inserted through the loop of a lead, at the end of which was a small dog, nose to the ground, stub tail stuck straight up, flicking back and forth in the air.

'I used to live nearby,' Benjamin Tate said.

'Right.' The old man hesitated, as if replaying in his mind

what had just been said to him. 'Well, it's a dark corner. Whether you live here or not.' He put out his hand. 'Here. Come away now.'

Benjamin Tate looked down the road. There was something there. He couldn't see what it was, but it was there. He looked back at the old man, pointing off into the dark. 'See?' he said. The old man, who still had his hand out, said something back but Benjamin Tate had stopped listening. He looked back down the road. In the brief moment he'd not attended it, it had crept closer, although it still couldn't be seen. Benjamin Tate leant forward from the hip, stretching out his neck. He was conscious of not wanting to move his feet. 'It's just over there. Can you see?' The dog was yapping silently on the end of its lead. The old man put a foot into the road and then withdrew it. His mouth was moving. The hand not holding the lead was gesticulating in the air. He looked angry. Benjamin Tate started laughing. Down the road the thing that was there was closer still. It had a shape now, a black, formless bulk. He only had to wait a moment longer and it would reveal itself to him.

Would Clare ever let him kiss her? What did it matter. He realised he didn't want to kiss her. For the first time he imagined her without any clothes on. How old was she? She had told him, but he'd forgotten. She would have been about Clare's age now. She. Yes, this was the spot. He felt sure of it now. They'd both been ended here. He would have to speak her name.

Suddenly the thing in the road began to charge. It moved with alarming speed towards him, gulping up the ground. He could hear a whirring sound. He wasn't sure if it was the thing itself, or the sound of the air being shoved aside in front of it. The small dog tried to leap away but the lead pulled taut, jolting its head back and sending its hindquarters flaying out in front of it. Two eyes, two dazzling eyes at the front of something monstrous coming at him, hurtling itself at him. He looked down at his feet, immobile. He didn't care. He had tried to kill himself many times. With rope. With pills. *Be brave.* But he was such a coward. He realised they were headlights at the same time he realised it was too late to get out of the way.

Just before they hit he saw the driver's face illuminated in the dashboard lights. It was his own face, younger, with sun on it, although there was no sun. Then the car was on top of him, crashing over him, ploughing through him, and he was tumbling backwards through empty space. The moon and the stars and the black road spun around him, faster and faster until they merged and he couldn't tell them apart. He saw himself with his arms folded across his chest, travelling at light-speed through a tunnel. He realised he'd run out of time. He began to shout out her name, but he was moving too fast now and the words were behind him before they were ever heard, like those white puffs of smoke that had once disappeared over his shoulder. Then, with one final whoosh, the tunnel ended, and he went spinning off into open space, like something rigid dropped out of the back of a plane.

'You crazy bugger!' The excited dog, he thought it was a terrier, reached him first. It jumped up onto his chest and began licking his face. He was surprised by how light the animal was. 'What the hell are you playing at?' The old man caught up, coughed. He looked flushed. Benjamin Tate stood up. The road, in both directions, was empty. He bent down and stroked the dog. The fur around its nose was hard and course. There was a white patch beneath its chin like a small goatee beard. 'Good boy,' he said. 'What a good boy.' He thought he'd like to get a dog. 'Sorry,' he said, addressing the old man now, but not looking at him, still stroking the dog. 'Just a dizzy spell.'

CHAPTER TWENTY-FIVE

Benjamin Tate looked at the fan, parts of the fan, smashed on the floor. He regretted it now. Where had this heat come from? It had sat on top of him, stagnant and thick, for days. He'd reach for something, stretch out an arm or extend himself in some other way, and bits of him would peel apart, like he'd been smeared with a paste that didn't dry. It was too early in the year for this. It was still spring, the tree was all made up but already it seemed to be wilting. 'I don't know what's happening either,' he said to it. When had the seasons started playing fast and loose with the natural order of things? Didn't they realise that order was there for a reason, that everything had its place, that one thing follows another thing and makes the next thing possible?

The poor fan, it had been all abuzz with giddy enthusiasm when he'd retrieved it from the airing cupboard, but almost immediately it became apparent that it was no longer fit for purpose. He contemplated it for a moment, watched it toil desperately back and forth in its cage, rattling annoyingly, continuously, coughing out gusts of hot air at whatever crossed its path, then he had picked it up and swung it against the wall.

The doddering old fool had died immediately of shock, but Benjamin Tate had continued swinging until its ribcage split open and its brittle innards splintered off in all directions. He had glared about then, seeking a next victim. He'd focused on the perfidious television – perhaps its hunchback, its deformity, is what made it so snide and resentful. He thought of the brassy number four with its impish, irreverent smirk. He imagined it on the floor jumping up and down as he pummelled it.

The fan wasn't an isolated case. Various bits of crockery, a cup, two plates, one breakfast bowl which had still been full at the time, had all met similarly abrupt and brutal ends in recent weeks.

These furious squalls that blew up in him now, they had caught him unawares. He lived now in an almost constant state of volatile unease. It's not what he'd expected. He'd expected instead a gentle return to peace and quiet, boredom, a safe, ordered progression through the days with no sudden movements. Just like before. But nothing was as before. Or, more to the point, everything was as before, and that was the problem.

It was Thursday. The crack-and-whip of the sheets wasn't quite as crisp as he'd have liked. He took the dressing gown and slippers off the stool and then wrestled with the hot tap in the kitchen while the kettle gurgled behind him. He sat down at the table. The brown shoes, the black ones, he hardly noticed. At 8.35 he slammed the door behind him, hearing the number rattle and shake on its hook as he descended the stairs. Would it never fall down?

The cat might have been there again, on that low wall, or it might not have been. Benjamin Tate walked with his head down, staring the entire way at the pavement a yard in front of him. The vast white building glared at him as he approached. His steps echoed down its stairway and at 8.56 – he must have been walking quicker than normal – he sat down at his desk.

Dunne, K. Thirty-six. He scanned down the list. All the normal things, along with a succession of broken bones. The clavicle, the humerus, the sacrum, the radius, the femur, the tibia and fibula, multiple ribs, carpals, metacarpals... Osteogenesis imperfecta. A collagen deficiency. Years ago, Benjamin Tate would have winced, going through that list, imagining the pain of each fracture. He'd seen it once, that man in the mud, balancing on the bank before momentum and gravity took him, or most of him. His oversized wellies had been sucked down, holding fast his feet to the spot. He'd teetered a moment, at an unlikely angle, until something gave way and he went crashing over. Benjamin Tate had laughed; the man's rain jacket had ridden up his back, tipping his hood over his face and exposing, above his belt, a slab of blotchy white skin. But then the screaming had started. Of course, each break is different, both by degree and location. Would a leg bone hurt more than any other? He remembered his own injury. It hadn't hurt at all at first. Then it had hurt a great deal. Poor K, whoever he or she was. He turned the card over. The entries stopped abruptly. Whoever he or she had been.

Chairs shuffled around him, voices, loud and then much softer, Pete laughing. Benjamin Tate kept his head down and continued working his way, diligently, reliably, fastidiously, through the cards. *Tap, tap, tap* went his fingers on the keys. *Tap, tap, tap*. The clock had been replaced. Next time he would be the one to throw it. Time moved ever on. At lunchtime, he made his way to the bench out the front, ate the sandwiches he'd prepared and looked alternately at the sky, the grass and the trees until the hour passed. At one point a man sat briefly beside him. When he stood up a bookmark fell from somewhere about his person. Benjamin Tate picked it up. It was a patch of material onto which the word '*daddy*' had been embroidered with three kisses beneath it. He put it in his pocket and watched the man walk away.

Dylan, B. Eighteen. More voices around him. One voice missing. Darren wasn't there. Damien rather. Pete and Sophia sat next to each other now. He noticed them, when he got up from his desk or returned to it, leaning into each other, murmuring things under their breaths, earnest things, playful things, exclusive things just between them. *Tap, tap, tap.*

At day's end he returned to his flat. Things were where he'd left them, where they were meant to be. The window was closed. Thursday was meat night, which offered him a great many options. Were there more types of edible meat than bones in the body? He'd have to look it up. He always had chicken. It was the most versatile of the meats, in his opinion. He did little with it that evening, just let it cook for ten minutes and then heated up some peas. He ate quickly at the table, taking little enjoyment from the dish. Then he washed up what he'd used, checked the water level in the kettle, and went to bed.

It was not yet 8pm, it was still light outside, but he didn't feel like reading, wasn't interested in watching television, or being watched by it. He stomped into his bedroom. It felt strange, retiring at such an hour. He kept the curtains open and stayed as still as he could, watching the sky change colour and darken like a bruise. Eventually it grew so dark he could see nothing of it at all, just a vast, depthless void that seemed to press against his window and then seep into and fill up his room, and he wasn't sure if he was even still awake.

Benjamin Tate was a boy again, he dreamed he was a boy again. He knew the house. It was a long way from where he was born but it is where his memories had begun. He saw himself standing in the kitchen. He had a dishcloth in one hand and a plate in the other. He can't have been more than six years old. The radio was on and his parents were dancing on the tiles in front of him, as they so often did. He and Charlie were watching them and making faces at each other but he certainly was warmed, reassured, by the sight. He saw his mother's bare feet, hard and cracked at the heel – she danced on tiptoes – and the way his father looked at her, with amusement and something else. It was longing, but he didn't know that then.

He saw the trunk of the great oak tree that split in two the wooden fence at the end of their garden, could feel again its cold surface, hard and smooth as stone. Who lived on the other side of that fence? A slight woman, but stern, who always wore dark-green slacks and industrial boots. He remembered her as being unfeasibly old – but then aren't all adults unfeasibly old when you're young – and that he'd been afraid of her. She used to let them, he and Charlie, hop over the fence and swing on her hammock. Onto the trunk his father had chalked three cricket stumps and they would all, his mother too, charge about late into the evening. He recalled the grass-itch on his legs when he climbed stickily into bed.

How dismal it was, reliving those days, knowing the wreck that was to become of them all.

<hr>

'What about your family?' Clare had asked him.

'I've a brother, but we're not in touch anymore.' Can you be estranged from a sibling?

'That's all?' she asked. 'Just a brother?'

His mother, untypically, had gone before his father, but then she had always been the instigator. She'd not been the same after the thing that had happened, she acted as though it happened to her somehow, and had developed dementia early in life, while still in her forties. He suspected, cruelly perhaps, but everyone was cruel for a while, that she'd gone there deliberately, that she was hiding.

He went to visit her in that desolate building with its misleadingly bright garden rimmed with benches and flowerbeds for as long as he could stand it, and had then given up the ghost – or given up on the ghost. His mother would gaze in his general direction, seeing nothing but the shape of a person. She'd look at him in turn indifferently, inquisitively, accusingly, which was when he thought she knew him best. She'd blurt out disconnected phrases, fragments of things that were impossible to piece together.

'Don't let it happen,' she said once, fearfully, fretfully. 'Promise me.'

He nodded at her but she grabbed his shoulders and shook them with surprising violence.

'No, you must promise me!' she shouted.

He said that he promised, and then leaned in to hold her, to offer comfort through the cage, but as soon as his arms opened, her face changed and she lashed out, catching him with a closed fist on the cheek. Her wedding ring had torn open the skin and he stood there, shocked, holding a hand to his face while she circled him warily, poised to strike again.

'Don't worry,' his father had said when they were walking back to the car. It was late afternoon and the sun had been especially bright, making his father's eyes water. 'She won't know the difference.'

Perhaps staying away after that had been the easy option. It hadn't felt easy. But then she'd died a few weeks later, considerately, falling down the stairs and breaking her neck, sparing him long nights of doubt and self-recrimination.

His father hadn't lasted much longer. The life-force had drained out of him the night the nursing home spoke to him in those tender, hushed tones and, after withering on the vine for a torturous six months, visibly shrivelling up from the outside in, he too broke off the stem and dropped to dust. The doctors named his disease to explain it to themselves, but Benjamin Tate knew it wasn't that, knew it was simple sorrow that he'd been unable to endure.

'Dad?' he said. They were alone in the too-big house and the old man was in his favourite chair. The television flickered in his open eyes as the room darkened and cooled around them. What had they been watching, an old western maybe. When the film ended those dazed, unblinking eyes had been open still. 'Dad?' he said again, not daring to look. The room was cold by then, a chill had settled on all the surfaces he wasn't touching. Then, much later, 'You've left me all alone.'

Where was Charlie in all of this? He was never there. Perhaps he had already gone to the city. What did he do there? Benjamin Tate never fully knew.

'Now we're finally equal,' Charlie had sneered at the funeral, their father's. Benjamin Tate had hobbled away without reply, too absorbed in his own grief, but the comment had snagged in his thoughts like a burr in a dog's coat and he'd carried it with him for a long time. He carried it still. Like so much else.

He recalled suddenly the night he'd packed up the house, discovered all that secret debris of lives interrupted. There were the love letters, hundreds of them, written over decades, from the time before they were married to the time just before the thing that had happened. There was a small ornamental elephant with a story behind it only the deceased knew, school reports, his, Charlie's, old photographs, birthday cards. He found, late one evening, the star that he'd placed on top of the Christmas tree as a boy. What was it doing in a kitchen drawer, among the batteries and the bike locks and the broken bits of things that wouldn't now be fixed? He'd picked it up and then sat down on the linoleum tiles, holding it in his lap for a long time.

Probably the hardest things to pack away were the clothes. There were grease stains in the collars of his father's shirts, strands of dyed blonde hair, his mother's, entwined in the wool of her cardigan. It was about 4am when Benjamin Tate noticed hanging behind the door his father's suit bag. He took it down off the hook. It was flimsy and light without the suit inside it. His father had only ever owned the one. It was navy blue, blue enough to appear black when required. He wore it to weddings, christenings, funerals, his wife's and his own. Something inside Benjamin Tate, at that point, had given way, and he'd rushed downstairs, to that same kitchen drawer, and returned with a black refuse bag into which he stuffed everything that had been stacked on the bed. An hour later that bag was slouched like a forsaken old dog on a doorstep in town, the neon sign above the charity shop blinking its thanks as he limped away.

He looked at the shattered television. When had that happened? How? But good. Good. The back end of a hardback stuck out through the last jagged shards. He thought of referred anger. Did it exist? Of course it did. He imagined most anger was in some way referred, caused by one thing, expressed on another. He was stupid to have left her like that. But who did he mean now? History repeats. *Be brave.*

The bench. *Stay.* The yellow car. The two bicycles. Had

there been a great silent bird up there somewhere, peering imperviously down? Or was he embellishing? What did it matter. Details. Mere details.

In the few remaining pixels of the television screen he could see the vague, muffled outline of his trousered legs. Maybe it did watch him after all. Something did. Maybe it was showing him now. Or warning him. *You're not a whole person. You're not really here. You're just a faint impression of a person.* He knew of creatures who existed only in the dark, at the bottom of oceans, in caves. These were anaemic, spectral beings that couldn't survive the light. He was among them again, had always been among them. A cave dweller, the ultimate cave dweller, hidden away, out of sight, growing dimmer and less present all the time until people passed through him, saw through him, without ever noticing, like he'd never even been there.

It was Thursday. Or it was the following Thursday? Or was it the Thursday after that? Recurring. That was the word, wasn't it, for these days? The crack-and-whip. The sheets had been changed and changed again. The brown shoes. The black shoes. The red door closing – slamming – behind him. *Tap, tap, tap.* The dim alleyways between the cabinets. Drawers that didn't shut pouncing out to crack his shins. All the names. All the people he'd never know, who'd never know him. The pavement beneath his feet. The cramped kitchen. The sky changing out of the window. The blackness creeping in and then creeping out. The dressing gown and slippers. Beginning it all again.

CHAPTER TWENTY-SIX

Clare was gazing vacantly in front of her. Without taking any of it in, her eyes passed in turn over the scrap of paper bent beneath the table leg, the table above it that fidgeted regardless, the menu that never changed. There was nothing very much on her mind. She was fortunate like that. It was Friday morning. There were two people in the café besides her; an old man who was seated at the unsteady table – thick languid drops of egg yolk dripped off it onto his grey slacks but he'd not noticed – and a man in a fluorescent-yellow jacket. Clare would not have been able to describe either of them. She was leaning forwards over the counter, resting on her elbows. Her chin was cupped in her hands and every so often she tipped her head forwards to allow a single finger to brush her fringe delicately out of her eyes. She had no idea that she was being watched.

Benjamin Tate would not have called it a lair, although from where he was he could see directly through the glass façade of the café while being fairly certain that anyone looking the other way would not have easily seen him. He had stumbled upon this spot by chance, when he had set off on the 749 steps that led to the café and stopped after 680 of them. At this time of the morning, it was now 8.43, the patch of grass between the path and the high wall was always in shade, and he'd discovered that if he stood very still against the bricks he would often be unnoticed even by the people walking past. Clare was there this morning. She hadn't always been. Twice he'd seen instead a much older lady behind the counter, her mother, he presumed, although there was no obvious resemblance; perhaps Clare was her father's daughter. Her hair was different. It had been cut and styled in a way that he thought quite caustic, shaved on one side, a fringe chopped angrily at an angle across her forehead. It didn't suit her, or rather it didn't suit the version of her he'd imagined for himself. It annoyed him, those hard edges, on something he wanted to be soft, but many things now annoyed him. He tried not to blame her and began walking.

Clare had been waiting for Benjamin Tate these past weeks without realising that's what she'd been doing, and without any particular emotion. Each time the door had swung open at about this time of day she had looked over expecting to see his sad figure poised there, and each time it had not been him she'd continued on exactly as before. She would not visit him. The conclusion she'd drawn about broken pipes still stood. It was his turn, or it was no one's turn.

It was a glorious morning, breathless and bright. He tried to imagine the world without people in it, with just the animals roaming around nibbling at the dewy grass. He wondered if it would be improved. At the kerb he stopped. A line of cars had been halted by something and were fuming impatiently and muttering beneath their breath. He looked up, watched for a moment a white line that was drawing itself arrow straight across a sky that was flat and blue and far away. *We're everywhere*, he thought. The cars still hadn't moved and he put his hand out, stepped into a narrow gap and sidled through it. Enough time had been wasted. He crossed the road. He was beneath the café sign. He was reaching forwards, grasping the metal handle that had caught the early sun and was warm to the touch.

'Well, well,' Clare said. Both customers glanced up, at her, at him, and then returned disinterestedly to their breakfasts.

He approached the counter. Behind her a coffee machine was clunkily realigning itself.

'Hello,' he said.

'And here I was thinking you were avoiding me.'

Since he'd started dreaming again one dream had kept recurring. It was less a dream and more a moment. He was on a mountainside. There was a thick, impenetrable fog all around him. High peaks reared up although he couldn't see them. They emphasised his smallness, or his isolation, he wasn't sure which. In front of him was a barely discernible dark shape. It seemed at first like the last glimpse of something departing, but he realised gradually that it was actually coming towards him, that what he believed to be its back was in fact its front, and he had only to remain where he was for a few seconds more and it would reveal itself to him. He always awoke then.

'I think I've been avoiding a lot of things,' he said.

Clare tilted her head and a large, hooped earring fell out of her hair and dangled on her shoulder. 'That sounds to me like the start of a much longer conversation.'

'Yes, maybe.' He looked at his watch. It was 8:52. He didn't want to be late. 'I wondered if you'd like to borrow any more books?' he said.

She smiled then. 'Yes. I'd like that.'

Benjamin Tate was sitting on the only chair in the room. The two identical cushions had been thrown off at various times long before then. He could only see one from where he sat. It was slumped against the wall. It had a rip in it through which a plume of padding bulged. He surveyed the room, the smashed television, the marks on the wall where various cups and bowls, some empty, some not, had shattered, the corner of the carpet that had been curiously ripped from its staples.

So much chaos. So much chaos and disorder it was actually astonishing. How had he managed it, he of all people? He looked down at his tummy, patted it. The patting became harder until he was rapping it with a closed hand. *Hello in there? Nothing to say for yourself?* The little tyrant had been mysteriously absent all these days. He'd waited for him to emerge from under his bridge, fists clenched and cheeks all aflush, he'd willed it even, the confrontation that would inevitably occur, he thought somehow it would be cathartic, defining even, but there had been no sign of him. He leaned across towards the table with the vague notion of pulling it over. His fingers brushed the wood but couldn't gain sufficient purchase and he sunk back into the cushions, disinclined to stand up. His poor mother. His poor dear dead mother. He started to chuckle. She would have been aghast at the state of this, she who had always been so house-proud, so fond of tidying up and putting away. His chuckle became a laugh. He was struck by the sound of it, fascinated almost, it was so strange to him. Abruptly he stopped. He looked at the door. Clare would come through it at any moment.

'Come on,' he said, banging his fist into the arm of the chair, 'hurry up.'

He'd been sitting there for three hours when finally he heard the stairs creaking. He jumped up and rushed across the room, swinging the door open before she even had a chance to knock.

'Hello,' he said, beckoning her in eagerly. 'You're here. Come in, come in.'

'Good Lord. What's come over you?' She had come straight from the café and was still wearing her black trousers and the blouse with her name badge pinned to it. 'Why are you grinning like that?'

She walked past him and then stopped. He wasn't sure why he wanted her to see his flat this way. There had been so much time, that day, the previous day, the days before that, to clean up, but he had deliberately not cleaned up. It was a challenge, or a confession, or both.

'Are you surprised?' he asked.

She put her hands on her hips but didn't answer him for a moment. Eventually she turned around. 'I am actually,' she said, 'I don't think I've ever seen you smile before.'

In the kitchen everything seemed to crowd in on him. It had been constricting lately, he was sure of it. Surely he'd not managed in here for twenty years. He thought of all the thousands of meals he'd prepared. Friday was pasta night. A cupboard swung out at him and he punched it away roughly, making it slap loudly against its frame. Where were all the cups? He looked at the sink, full of a grey liquid. He dipped his hand into it. It was cold and as he rummaged about soft things floated against his arm. Eventually he hooked two cups and dried them hastily on his shirt. There was a teaspoon on the floor and he plucked it stickily away from the tiles.

'The milk is off,' he said when he returned. 'It's black tea.'

She was perched on the edge of the chair. He noticed then a trail of something down its back. Whatever it was had crusted over and had lumps in it. He tried to recall what they might be, how they had got there. He wondered vaguely if some of it had transferred to his clothes in the hours he'd been seated there.

'I like what you've done with the place,' she said.

He put the two cups on the table. Ah, there was the second cushion, cowering between its legs. He kicked it idly.

'You weren't going to come back, were you?' he asked.

'Honestly? No.'

'That's fine. Just as well I came to the café, then.'

She held open her hand. In her palm were a dozen or so staples that she'd pulled out of the floorboards.

'Why did you come back?' she asked. She stood up then and walked the few paces to the television set, carefully retrieving the hardback book that protruded out of it. More glass crumbled to the carpet. 'To give me this?'

She handed the book to him and he took it automatically without looking at it. It was heavier than he remembered. It had seemed as nothing when he'd snatched it off the shelf and hurled it at the hunchback's smirking face.

'I've been so angry,' he suddenly said, surprising himself.

She took the book from him and slid it back into its final resting place. 'I can see that,' she said. 'I'm sorry. I really didn't mean to give you the wrong impression.'

'What?' For a moment he didn't understand. *Oh, the canal.* She meant the canal. It seemed so remote now, so frivolous. *Don't flatter yourself,* he thought nastily, before checking himself. Referred anger. *Don't blame her.* 'No, that was my fault. I didn't mean that.'

'Oh.' She seemed for a fraction of a second almost affronted. Her fringe fell into her eyes and she brushed it away with that same delicate finger. 'What then? Has something else happened?'

All at once he realised what all this was about, why she had come, not just that day, but in the first place. The realisation made him gasp. He'd never spoken of it, the thing that had happened, he didn't know how to.

'Yes,' he said, 'something else did happen.'

Her face changed. She'd not been expecting that and sat back down now. The staples were still in her palm and she tipped them casually onto the floor between her feet then folded her hands in her lap. She looked up at him. 'Go on then.'

He felt suddenly light-headed and reached for the table to steady himself. The old tree was there, just in front of him. He could see its face again, a kind face, grave but kind. It was willing him on.

'There was a girl,' he managed.

'Yes, there usually is.'

He shook his head. Not like that. He hadn't meant it like that.

'What was her name?' Clare asked.

He looked beyond the tree at the sky that was still blue and flat and far away. What was her name? When did he first discover it? Who had told it to him? He'd read it many times, on hospital forms, in newspapers, but he was sure someone had told him it before then. What if he'd never known it, would it have been easier, more impersonal? What was her name? Such a simple question. But she had no idea what she asked of him. He thought suddenly he would be sick. His tummy spat something up and it singed the back of his throat. He closed his eyes. Her name was... Her name was... Just like that. He knew her name. Why could he not speak it, even silently?

'Her name was Madeline,' he said. *Oh, so close. Next time.* Hands that had been gripping the table's edge relaxed and released it. He noticed his knuckle was bleeding where he'd punched the cupboard.

'Pretty name.'

'She'd have hated you.'

'Oh. That's nice.'

'She wasn't nice.'

Poor Madeline. Ever the distraction. He'd used her then. He used her now. *'Daddy's little princess.'* That's what she'd have said about Clare. He could hear her saying it, spitting out the words with such malice. He remembered once how she had grown sullen one afternoon when they'd been paging through a magazine together. He'd commented casually about an actress he'd liked. She'd said nothing for a long time before suddenly snatching the magazine out of his hand, ripping out the offending page and then, quite impressively, eating it right there in front of him. With her mouth still clogged and chewing she said something about faces – or faeces – nothing surprised him.

'She wouldn't have hated you really,' he said. 'She'd have been jealous of you. It would have just looked like hate.'

'Why jealous?'

He ignored her. It was irrelevant. She asked him something else and he ignored that too. It was all irrelevant. It was just stalling. *Be brave.* The tree was still watching him, waiting.

'Forget Madeline,' he blurted. 'It's not about her.'

Clare stood up, took a tentative step towards him. Glass crunched beneath her shoes and she hesitated. 'Who is it about then?' she asked.

He was on the road. He was on the roundabout, swinging round it. He was going too fast. But had he been going too fast? He never knew. They had been so desolate, her parents, when he had stumbled upon them at the graveside. They were his burden too. Huge tears suddenly. He turned away, seeking solace, but it was just a tree now. He crunched his lids together. There was a hand on his shoulder. It squeezed lightly then withdrew.

'When you're ready,' Clare said, 'you tell me.'

'I can't tell you. But I can show you.'

CHAPTER TWENTY-SEVEN

They met early the next morning. She was waiting for him at the end of his road. The cool air had flushed her cheeks and coloured her lips and given her a fresh-out-of-the-box appearance, all health and natural goodness.

'I wasn't sure you'd come.' Either of them might have said that.

They walked together through the town at a time when it was still empty, while the shops were still closed and the drunks still slumped in their doorways. His knee ached. It always ached in the morning, but it had ached more so since its altercation with the bin. It had stiffened up around the joints and when he climbed up or down stairs sharp shocks fizzed along his tendons. The pain made him walk awkwardly, more awkwardly, with an ungainly list and lurch that he was self-conscious of; he saw it, in his shadow, loping on the paving stones in front of him. Pigeons flocked around them, hopping from foot to scraggy foot, jabbing beaks into the cracks. Every now and then one would jump up in the air and flap its wings at them before settling down a yard further away.

They walked on, away from the centre and into the back

alleys, the dirty gullies where teenagers and feral cats roamed with equal enmity. There was the bin tipped over, its contents half spewed out and already picked through; there was the garage door upon which someone had scratched their slogans and secret symbols; there was the wooden gate hanging open to reveal an unkempt garden, cluttered with junk – a sofa, a fridge, other incongruous items. All that waste. Those who lived here weren't impoverished, not really, despite their best efforts to look the part. They were, despite their mutterings, among the most asset-rich people on the planet, and in the history of humankind. *Yes*, he thought, *the world would be better without people in it.*

'Where are you taking me?' Clare asked, a little uneasily.

'It's not far.'

The derelict part of town ended suddenly, at a wide road. On the other side a barren, windswept field rolled up to the crest of a hill upon which a thicket of trees stood stark against the pale sky. Within it, invisible from where they stood, was a church, around which, dug into the turf, this year, last year and a hundred years hence, neglected and not neglected, were dozens of gravestones. She was buried beneath one of them. She. Would he never speak her name?

'That way?' Clare asked, looking up the slope.

The weak sun was in front of them and they squinted into it. He didn't belong where he was taking her. It wasn't his place. As they drew closer the church steeple gradually began to show itself through the foliage.

'Oh,' Clare said, 'I didn't even know...' Her voice trailed off into a silence that deepened around them, that went beyond not talking. It was much cooler under the trees, still damp from the night. Sodden leaves wrapped themselves around roots. A squirrel stopped, registered their presence without looking at them, scampered erratically up a trunk in long spirals. They walked on and as abruptly as they'd entered the wood they emerged from it, arriving into a secluded glade. For a moment they stood soundlessly on its edge, adjusting to the stillness, the deathly hush. It felt like everything, the air, the grass, the critters who spent their days fussing amongst the undergrowth and the fallen things, had frozen suddenly at their intrusion, and the silence echoed with things unfinished, interrupted. Amidst it all, in the centre of this secret world, stood the church, sentient, solemn, vigilant.

'This way,' he said, or whispered, or only thought, and set off between the gravestones, where the grass was flattened like deer-track. He hadn't gone far into the graveyard when he stopped abruptly. He stared down at one of the headstones with a puzzled expression. He dropped to his haunches to read the inscription more clearly, to be certain, and then stood up again. He looked at the headstone beside it, and then on its other side. He looked at Clare, who titled her head at him questioningly.

'It's been so long,' he explained.

Then he was off again. He'd only gone a few steps when he stopped suddenly for a second time, turned around, read the name etched into the stone. She read it too, looking for different things. He stood up.

'No,' he said, growing agitated now. 'I thought I knew it. It must be here.' He walked on, quicker this time, and this time she let him go, watching him zigzag back and forth, stop, retrace his steps, set off again in a different direction. The sun had crested the trees now and a hazy, yellowish mist hung about them.

As he paced she looked up at the white-blue sky; days often started like this, in hopeful, clear-headed sunshine. She hoped it would last. Perhaps they were in the wrong place. Perhaps he'd misremembered whatever it was he was trying to remember. She yawned in a deep, satisfying way, and put her hand to her head, feeling the bristles where her hair had been shaved. It was still novel. She hadn't liked it at first, the cut, it had seemed too severe, but it was growing on her.

She realised that he had stopped pacing. He was on the far side of the cemetery and she made her way to where he stood. There were fresh flowers on the bright white tablet at his feet, and the grass around it had been meticulously cut. She read the name, and the two dates beneath it. *'Taken too soon.'* She looked at the dates again. How old was he? He must have been very young. 'Your daughter?' she eventually asked.

He looked at her quickly. It hadn't crossed his mind that she'd think that. But it was the obvious conclusion. He wondered if that would have made it easier or more difficult. He thought easier. He would, he knew absolutely, he would have followed her by now.

'I killed her,' he said.

They had just been outlines at first, her parents, just black shapes of people against the church but he knew immediately it was them. It was a year afterwards. To the day. He had watched from a distance. She had been kneeling down, or not kneeling, crouching, bent right over, arms and face pressed to the ground, in the same attitude she'd adopted on the road. He was standing behind her, very still, looking over his wife's head towards something that wasn't there, was no longer there. What is it about grief that singles people out, that makes others spot it in them when there are no obvious outward signs? Wherever they went, this couple, whatever they were doing, their pain would show through and pull them apart from the people around them. Finally she had stood up and placed herself alongside her husband, and they remained there, not moving. He had noticed from his shadowed spot beneath the branches that they were not touching, that between them there was an empty space that they had not noticed or not been inclined to close.

He took a graceless step forward – graceless in so many ways. His leg then was still unrepaired, unbending; he would require two further operations in the coming months. Like them, he was also maimed. Neither had turned as he approached, and he'd closed to within five yards without them hearing him or sensing his presence. Whatever place he had sent them to, they were alone there. When they did eventually turn around they stopped and stared at him in disbelief, as though he were another of the ghosts they had been in such recent communion with. Benjamin Tate – for he was by then Benjamin Tate, Ben had gone – watched the shock of recognition come to their faces. He realised he should not have been there and bowed his head. Through the blades of grass an earthworm was painstakingly at work submerging itself in the soil. It undertook the task in stages, extending its inner layer before its outer layer rippled after it. Which end was which?

'It's you.'

Benjamin Tate looked up again. It appeared as if the father had been holding his breath for a long time. Something behind his eyes was straining outwards making them bulge. He recognised him then as the same man he'd seen running in the park, the pot-bellied slogger he'd mocked and taunted with his splendid, athletic body, and the same man he'd spoken to in the playground days later. He realised suddenly who was beneath them. Maybe she'd been so light because she was almost gone.

Benjamin Tate couldn't speak, but mouthed the two words he'd said to them before, as feeble and small as they were in the face of this great monstrosity. The father had shaken off his wife's restraining hand and stepped forward. Benjamin Tate thought he was going to punch him, had hoped he was.

'I wish it was me,' he said.

'So do I.'

Clare was holding on to him now. They were still in the cemetery. She was talking softly, her mouth close against his ear. She told him it would be all right, that he mustn't blame himself, that it was so long ago and that it was a mistake, just a mistake, and everyone makes mistakes. She said other things. He didn't hear them all. He realised he must have told her how it had happened. He didn't remember when. She said that time would heal, that Ruby would be with her parents again one day. Would she, though? He wasn't sure. How would that work? People often said that at such times, that we'll find our loved ones in the afterworld, and that all our broken families would be put back together again. It was a comforting idea, and he'd tried to believe it, but it had never made sense to him. Which families would be put back together? The families of our childhood, or of our – or their – parenthood? Who would claim us? Are we forever to be cast as our parents' children, or our children's parents? Somewhere the chain must break.

The man beside her on the bed had his eyes closed. He had been talking for hours. A lot of what he'd said made no sense to her. It didn't matter; she didn't think he was talking to her. She had been shocked by what he'd confessed earlier in the day, a little repelled even. She didn't blame him, felt incredible sympathy for him, for the burden he had carried, was carrying still. And yet... And yet. And yet something disgusted her. It was the act itself. And the act was a part of him. She wanted to know the details and was shocked by her morbid curiosity. She wanted to know if the girl, Ruby, had gone beneath the car or if the car had simply bumped her aside, and, if the former, had he felt her slip under his wheels. She'd driven over a daydreaming bird once. She had assumed it would fly away at the last moment, as they always did, but it had not moved. She remembered the sound it had made, the clean, quick thrump, like something disappearing down a drain. She hadn't expected the little mite to even register. She wanted to know if there was much blood, and if the mother had looked at him afterwards. What had she said? Had she said anything? What could she have said? It was her fault, too.

What was he saying now, something about a book, a beautiful book. What book? *Jonathan Livingston Seagull*? The one in the television? Clare was only half-listening. The curtains were closed although it was still daytime. She realised this was the first time she'd been in his bedroom. It was awful, even in this dim light. There was nothing in it. Like there had been nothing in the rest of his flat. There were the slippers and dressing gown neatly placed on the stool, but there was nothing else to suggest a real person occupied this space. How had he spent twenty years here and left no mark?

No, it wasn't the book that was beautiful, it was the bookmark, the bookmark that had fallen out of it. 'Good,' she said to him softly, stroking his brow, letting him blow himself out. 'That's good.'

Suddenly his eyes pinged open and he stared at her. 'It wasn't mine,' he said, 'but I took it. It was so special, and I took it.'

CHAPTER TWENTY-EIGHT

The curtains were open now and the room half lit by a milky-grey sky in the window. It could have been morning or evening, Benjamin Tate didn't know which, or care. He felt like he'd been asleep for a thousand years – not asleep, stupefied. He rose groggily and lumbered along the hallway. Faint traces of Clare's perfume sweetened the air, otherwise, so feverish and broken were his recollections, he'd have doubted the whole thing had ever happened.

In the doorway to the living room – such an ironic term for that place – he gazed listlessly on the things about him. He was indifferent to them now. They were just things. They were just there. He wondered at the energy it had taken to break so many of them. He had none of it left. He walked to the open window and leaned out. The tree was so close he could almost reach out and touch it. He leaned out further, then further again, he could lean out too far if he wanted, if he was brave enough. But no, it wasn't yet finished. He pulled himself back inside and sat heavily down on the carpet. How exhausting it had been, ignoring the thing that needed to be acknowledged and then finally dredging it up. His bones ached, and his skull, like it had been bruised on the inside by what had battered its way out. He looked at the carpet around him, imagined himself rolling over and closing his eyes. He might never open them again.

But the finish line doesn't come to meet you. Grudgingly he climbed back to his feet, steadying himself against the wall while the dizziness passed, and then walked into his bedroom to retrieve the ledger from the drawer. He read and then reread the address that was scrawled on the last page until he was confident he'd memorised it. Good old Pete. He always knew people, or knew people who knew people. In the kitchen the sink was still full, and he felt beneath the oily water until he found what he was looking for – yes, this would do, this would do nicely – and then put on his coat.

One final effort. A last hurrah. Telling Clare hadn't been the end he'd hoped for, but it had at least created the momentum that would lead to the end. At the door he paused and looked back into his flat. He didn't think he'd return. A shiver ran down his spine. If not, it would be for the best. Whatever happened it would be for the best. He could not, he would not, live through another day like the thousands that had gone before.

It was nearly dark when he entered the street he'd been searching for. It was wide, the thin trees that lined its pavements were taller than the lamp-posts, behind them on each side vast lawns – elegant, soft, strangely aloof – unfurled themselves to lay at the feet of grand well-lit houses. Discreet lights hidden beneath hedges or atop walls turned on as he passed, throwing ghostly shadows around him, lighting up in yellow hues the underside of leaves. Number two. Number four. Woodlands. The Haven. Not everywhere is confident enough to give itself a name. Number twelve. Number fourteen. At the next house he stopped, taking in the gables, the bay windows. Was it Victorian, Edwardian, a modern imitation of either? It wasn't what he'd expected, although he'd not have been able to say what exactly he had expected.

A pebbled walkway led away from the gate into a garden now black, like water at night. He started down it and a spotlight in the turf suddenly glared up at him, momentarily blinding him and vanishing all else behind a kaleidoscope of colours. At the porch a second light, softer, more tactful, turned on to reveal the white panelled door and the gold-leaf knocker. It was deceptively heavy in his fingers, and the dense, metallic sound it made against the door echoed through the small space where he now stood. He wondered if he would be recognised. How would he introduce himself if not? He realised he may be at the wrong house entirely, that the information he'd been given might be incorrect or out of date. Either way, this was as far as it went for Benjamin Tate, or this version of him at least.

He knocked again, waited, stepped off the porch and glanced up at the window where a light shone behind the curtains. Perhaps they were out after all. Was it Saturday night, or Sunday? He had already decided to wait indefinitely when the door finally opened.

The old man standing there looked at Benjamin Tate with blank, expressionless eyes.

'It's you,' he said. 'You finally came then.'

'You're not surprised?'

'I'm surprised it's taken so long.' He turned then and shuffled in that familiar way back into the house. Benjamin Tate followed him down the hallway. To his left and right the walls were almost completely covered with pictures of her. Some had been blown up to poster size, some, most, overlapped in montages that looked haphazard but were anything but. All the hours he'd taken, cutting them, shaping them, arranging and rearranging them, removing them and then, years later, retrieving them from the box and sliding them again behind the glass. There she was as a baby, on a high chair with food around her mouth and on her fingers and a haughty, defiant look upon her upturned face; there she was, older now, on the beach, on a grey day, bent forwards, head thrown back and hair blowing, laughing, laughing in that unbridled way that children do, children and blessed adults who keep the inner child alive; there she was, gap-toothed and beautiful, astonishingly beautiful, revealing the woman she'd have been, but mournful also, profound even, as she gazed away at something unseen. What was it about these pictures, all of them together, the collective, that bothered him?

The hallway opened into an enormous room, larger perhaps than his whole flat. Tim was on the opposite side of it, pouring drinks. His hand was shaking. The neck of the bottle trembled against the rim of the glass. It was the only sound in the room, that brittle high-pitched tinkling.

'I wasn't sure you'd recognise me,' Benjamin Tate said from the doorway.

'But how could I not recognise you? You must know I see you every night.'

Tim put the two glasses down on the table and lowered himself into a deep leather chair. He sunk into it easily and Benjamin Tate imagined he had spent many hours in that position.

'Sit,' he said, pointing to the chair opposite.

Benjamin Tate crossed the room and sat down. Between them, on the glass table, faint images of each man stared up tensely. For many moments then neither spoke as they came to terms with the other's presence. For more than two decades they had been intrinsically linked by a shared experience. They had each in their own way obsessed about the other, lived out this moment in their heads and wondered whether it would ever come to pass.

'So, here we are.'

'In the end I couldn't not come.'

Benjamin Tate looked around, taking in the vast room. So much space. Almost too much space. Yes, his entire flat would comfortably fit in here. A deep burgundy rug covered much of the polished wood floor. A gigantic mirror – how had they manoeuvred it through the door? – showed the two men again, seated quietly, in a parallel dimension. They might have been friends there. There was a fireplace, leather sofas, modern colour schemes and plush décor. He thought sourly of his own home, so bleak and meagre by comparison.

Tim drained the last of his drink and then leaned back. He put his head against the cushion and closed his eyes. For a moment he softly hummed to himself and then fell silent. He might have been asleep were it not for his finger tapping on the glass. *Tap, tap, tap* it went. *Tap, tap, tap.* So satisfied. So untroubled. *Good for him, though,* Benjamin Tate thought, *good for him. But also, fuck him. While I've been enduring the unendurable he's been living here, building an empire. It doesn't matter. Who am I to be bitter? The triumph of the world has no bearing on the failure of the individual, as convenient as it might be to think so.*

'You've done well for yourself,' he said.

'I've been successful,' Tim answered. 'Is that the same thing? I don't know. What about you? I noticed you limping. Is that still from then?'

'Yes. My knee.' He put a hand to it subconsciously. 'It's nothing.'

Tim nodded. 'So, there was no scholarship then.'

Scholarship? Good Lord, was that even the same life? It was

hard to fathom. The word came from a past so distant and removed that it was almost impossible to believe it had ever existed. But it had once. He had lived in it once, been its star, and once upon time so much had been in front of him.

'No,' he said now. 'No scholarship.'

'That's a shame. What have you done instead?'

'Nothing. I've done nothing. Actually, that is something I've been thinking a lot about lately.'

'Have you, indeed?' Tim smiled to himself. He had finished his drink and was halfway through another. 'An existential crisis. Poor you,' he added, closing his eyes again.

Benjamin Tate studied him closely. He appeared so much older than he'd expected. He'd allowed for the passage of time, added the years and created an impression of what he thought he might look like, but this decrepit figure was nothing like what he'd seen in his mind's eye. The spotlight was above and in front of him, glaring down on his face from a height. A reading light, he realised. Yes, he had surely spent many evenings in just this pose. The light was not flattering. It deepened and darkened shadows that he imagined were already deep and dark. And bald as a coot, too, with lips that had all but vanished, and those creases on his face. They made his skin look like a sheet of paper that had been screwed up and flattened out again.

He wanted to tell him that he wasn't in crisis, not of the existential kind or any other. It had been resolved, or very soon would be. He thought of his dream, of the dark shape that was approaching. He wasn't scared. Or he was a little scared. He put his hand on his thigh. The object was still tucked up tightly against it. It would come out soon enough.

'I hope you're up to it,' he said.

Tim opened his eyes again. 'What's that?' He refilled his drink, noticed Benjamin Tate's was still untouched and leaned forward, nudging it across the table towards him. 'Please, drink,' he said.

But he didn't want to drink. He wondered why he was even being offered a drink. He began to feel like something was slipping through his fingers, like he was being cheated in some undefinable way. He hadn't come here for this, to find solace in some sort of uneasy survivor's bond. Is that what was being offered?

'Are you married?' Tim asked.

'No.'

'Ever been?'

'No.'

'No. Something like this can isolate you, can't it?'

'I've got no one to blame but myself. Where's your wife tonight?'

Tim's finger froze on the glass. Was that a smile, a trace of a smile? 'Well, time really has stood still, for us, hasn't it? My wife is no longer my wife. Not for years.' He waved his glass dismissively, spilling much of it on the rug. He either didn't notice or didn't care. 'It was inevitable,' he continued. 'Husbands and wives rarely survive the death of a child.'

Benjamin Tate was shocked. That phrase. How could he say it like that, so casually, so matter of fact? Had he no heart? But it had been there all the time, circling. It had crept closer, snuck up stealthily, hiding behind other things, less diabolical things, and then leaped out into plain sight. It couldn't now be ignored. *The death of a child.* The fact of it sat there on the table like a hideous thing, like a horned beast, like the devil himself.

Tim got up and went to the drinks cabinet again. He refilled his glass, drained it, refilled it again. Was that his fourth, or fifth? He was nearly drunk. He brought a new bottle back with him and slouched heavily into his chair, groaning as he did so. His finger began ticking again. *Tap, tap, tap.*

Benjamin Tate tried to recall what had been written on his card. 'I won't read it,' he had promised Pete, 'I just want the address.' But Pete hadn't cared, and of course he'd read it. Depression, and something to do with his spine, something degenerative and chronic, and substance abuse. Had it just been alcohol?

Of course, all these delights had still been in front of him when they'd met first, half met. He had been just the slogger in the park then, and just the parent in the playground with sleep in his eye and a small child, his daughter – *the death of a child, say her name* – watching him from the foot of the slide with that churlish look on her face. How light she'd been. It was a marvel. And there they go now, hand in hand, with the early morning sun on them, disappearing together over the soft dew-covered verges. What had they talked about that day, that final day, on their way home? What do fathers and daughters ever talk about? They had so little time left.

'I've never spoken of it,' he said.

Why hadn't he? It angered him that his parents had never discussed it, not once, not to him at least. They must have talked endlessly amongst themselves during those long nights when he was still in the hospital. Yet their reticence when he'd returned had been almost abnormal. He'd first assumed they were simply giving him space in which to recover, in all manner of ways, but the days went by, the weeks went by, and then one morning he awoke with the knowledge that, without anyone noticing, a point had been passed and it could no longer be broached even if they'd wanted to.

Tim was watching him with steady, inscrutable eyes. 'That's because it's unspeakable,' he said, 'what you did.' He sat forward in his chair. 'I have an idea, why don't you tell me why you're really here tonight.'

Benjamin Tate's pulse quickened. 'Don't you know?'

'You tell me.' He picked up Benjamin Tate's full glass and plonked it back down clumsily on the table. 'I said drink.'

Benjamin Tate stared at it. The lights were dancing in its gold liquid. How were they, when nothing else in the room was moving? 'I don't want to have a drink with you,' he said. 'That's not what I want.'

'What do you want then?'

'I want what you owe me.'

'What I owe you? What can I possibly owe you? I owe you nothing.'

'Of course you do. You know what I did.' He suddenly realised what had bothered him about the photos in the hallway. They were all of the child, exclusively of her. In none of them was there a trace of either parent.

'Yes,' Tim said. 'And?'

'And nothing. Isn't that enough? Isn't what I did enough?'

'Enough for what?'

'Enough to pay me back. To need to pay me back.'

Tim was grimacing now. No, not grimacing, it was a smile. He was twitching. A vein in his temple pulsed. That hand, still trembling. Nerves. But not made nervous by this. No. Made nervous by life, his life, all of life. 'You need to tell me what happened,' he said.

'What?'

'I want to know.' He drained another glass, watching Benjamin Tate through the bottom as he did so. It bulged and distorted his eye. 'Tell me. Come on. Only you know. Talk me through it.'

That vile devil who had barged in on them jumped up. *The death of a child.* It reared up to its full height and started doing an appalling jig. Benjamin Tate stared at it, unable to tear away his eyes.

'I'm waiting,' Tim said. 'Don't make me keep imagining it. You say I owe you. Well, that's what you owe me.'

Benjamin Tate was shaking his head. *No, no, no.* He could not, would not go back there.

'But you must,' Tim said. He lifted the second bottle above his head, shook out the last drops onto his tongue. 'You must. It was such a lovely day. It was such a lovely fucking day. Explain to me how it could have possibly happened. You're in the car. You're driving…'

It was happening in front of him, right in front of him. He was watching it happen and he was powerless to prevent it. It wasn't a memory or a vision or something imagined. It was the actual thing, happening now, again, as it happened then. He knew this, for what else is the devil if not our deepest fears revealed? He saw the pushchair. He saw the bonnet. He saw the kerb and the small rubber wheel slipping off it. He saw her. She was there. She was there and then she wasn't there. It happened again, and again. It would go on, into perpetuity. He couldn't stand to look anymore. He put his head down.

'It has to end,' he said. The finish line doesn't come to meet you. His hand against his thigh pressed hard until the sharp edge began to cut into his skin.

'But it can't end. I can't let it end. If it ends she's gone forever. I'm her father. Have you forgotten that?'

'So, act like it.'

There was a wail then, a howl rather, it was animal. It shook the walls and made the windows rattle in their frames. Benjamin Tate looked up. Tim was standing above him. His hands were raised. The second bottle was in one of them. He bowed his head and waited. He thought again of his recurring dream, of the dark shape that was here now. It was huge and heavy and right on top of him. It would blot him out.

The bottle smashed near to his feet and then there was

silence. He waited. He looked up again. Tim was seated. His eyes were closed. He looked so still he might have suddenly died.

'Tim?' he said. It was the first time he'd used his name. It sounded awful in his mouth. 'Hello?'

Tim opened his eyes finally and stared at him. 'It's over. Get out.'

But it couldn't be over. This was the moment. He'd dreamed it. Benjamin Tate reached under the waistband of his trousers and withdrew the knife. It was long, serrated, deadly sharp. There was already blood on the blade. Tim looked at it with vague alarm and then closed his eyes again.

'I'm not sure you can handle two of us on your conscience, but so be it.'

'No,' Benjamin Tate said, 'it's for you. I brought it for you. It's my knife, so you can say I came here with intent. Take it.'

Tim didn't move.

'Please,' Benjamin Tate said. 'Please. It's my penance. Only you can do it.'

Tim leaned forward and took the knife. He sunk back into his chair. He looked groggily at his empty glass on the table, at the empty bottle at his feet and the smashed one in front of him. He craned his neck to look at the cabinet, at all the bottles lined up there. Too far. Too lazy. He sighed heavily, stared blindly into space. For a long time, he didn't speak.

'She used to sit on my lap,' he eventually said, 'in the mornings, when I couldn't sleep. Somehow, she always knew when I woke up. She used to come downstairs with her hair sticking up and snuggle up in my lap.' He shook his head. His hand moved as if she were there again and he was stroking her. 'She was so small. Her whole body could fit on my legs. The way she looked at me sometimes then. Like she was taking care of me, not the other way around. I'm sure she knew. I don't know how she did. But I've always been sure she knew what was coming.'

Benjamin Tate had sunk right back in his chair. He was only half listening. He was back on the roadside. The dark shape was receding from him. It was nearly out of sight and he'd been left behind. The fog was closing in again. He would be lost in it forever.

'How did you find me?' Tim asked. He waved the knife around. 'Here, I mean.'

Benjamin Tate lifted his eyes. 'What?' he managed.

'How did you get my address?'

'The surgery. I work there.'

Tim smiled ruefully. 'As easy as that. I've been trying to find you myself. For years I've been looking. You're right. I did have half a mind to kill you. For revenge, in her honour, all that rubbish. I didn't really want to kill you. I've just realised that. I only wanted to want to.' He threw the knife on the table. It slid across the glass and dropped onto the rug. 'Where do you live, what road?'

'Dean Street.'

Tim chuckled softly then, as if to himself. 'I've been nowhere near.' He closed his eyes. 'Put the knife away. I don't hate you. I hate what happened. There's a difference.'

<hr>

Tim picked up the phone and dialled. He waited. Eventually she answered and he heard her tone change when she realised it was him. Yes, he knew it was late, yes, he knew her children were asleep, yes, he'd promised after the last time to never call her again.

'Please, Beth, I have to show you something. You can never see me again after this if you want.'

An hour later she arrived at the church. Soft yellow lights on the outside walls, great depths of blackness all around them, the gentle nattering of nature in the land. She thought, as she always did when she came here, how peaceful a place it was to spend eternity. Even in this eerie light the tranquillity soothed her. She saw him standing by the grave and approached with curiosity and, she realised, caution.

He's killed him, that was the first thing she thought when he called her. He'd been searching for him for years. She'd never taken it seriously. But perhaps she had misjudged his intent. Perhaps he had finally tracked down the boy – but, no, he'd be a man now – and taken revenge. She had always believed that only death would finally end it. She had assumed she'd meant Tim's death, but saw now that the boy's death would have worked just as well.

'Thank you for coming,' he said.

'What did you want to show me?'

'My face,' he said, stepping forward into the light. 'Look. It's different?'

'What are you talking about, Tim? You look the same.'

'No. No, you're wrong. I'm not the same. Not at all. I'm something completely different now. I can't believe it.'

He started laughing, manically laughing. Beth stepped back. He was deranged. He'd finally gone mad. She was convinced now he'd killed the boy.

'I'm going,' she said, edging back further. 'Don't ever call me again.'

'No, wait.' He lunged forward and grabbed her shoulder. 'Don't you see? It's over. It's over, Beth. After all this time.'

'What is?'

'All of it.'

'You're not making any sense, Tim.'

'He came to see me. That's what I've been trying to tell you. Tonight. Out of the blue. He turned up on my doorstep. Can you believe it?'

'I knew it,' she said. 'What happened? What did you do to him?'

'Oh, Beth,' he said, and suddenly he flung his arms around her and held her so tightly, so tightly that she struggled for breath. He was laughing again. No. He wasn't laughing, he was crying. His face was buried in her hair and he was sobbing uncontrollably. She realised he'd not cried afterwards. How was that possible? Had he never cried? Had the poor man held onto this for so long? He was saying something now, but it was difficult to make out the words. She put her hands on his shoulders and held him in front of her.

'Stop,' she said. 'Stop and tell me.'

'He came to see me, Beth. And I forgave him. I forgave him.'

CHAPTER TWENTY-NINE

Benjamin Tate woke early, before his alarm. The softness of the mattress, the crack-and-whip of the sheets – he hardly noticed any of that; he was already up and out of bed. He strode down the hallway into the kitchen, looked at the coffee in the cup, the kettle filled just so, strode out again. No time. No time now, for that. He showered and dressed, the black shoes – he smiled at himself putting them on – and before eight o'clock, the red wooden door had been closed behind him.

Streaks of cloud in the sky, some yellow all through, some yellow only on the outside with grey middles – soft grey, not rain grey. They hung up there, high and distant and unmoving, but in another moment they'd have vanished. Much nearer, small wispy clouds had been hurrying low over the rooftops, rushing towards something, or from it. He preferred to think the former. He passed the bus stop, the low wall, no cat this time. 749 steps. He was fairly skipping over them.

Maybe it had been as simple a thing as sharing it, maybe that had made this difference. She had told him – how many times? – that it hadn't been his fault, that he didn't need to punish himself, that it was over, over, over. Maybe just hearing it. No one, he realised, had said those things to him before. Something had burst. *I forgive you.* Is this how other people felt?

Yes! There it was! The cat, trotting alongside him on the grass, tail and head in the air, flouncing daintily on the tips of its paws. *Hello, old friend.* Maybe it was a different cat. It didn't matter. How loud were the birds in the hedges? Was it just one bird, or many? He stopped to peer in. A dark shape hopped away from him. Why did he notice these things? He had always thought it was borne out of a desire always to escape himself, but what if it was something else, something magical? There was a morning not long ago when Benjamin Tate had resolved to be bright and new; he did so again, and this time he meant it.

The glass front of the café was ablaze in the early sunshine. It glinted at him as he approached. He swung open the door, felt the sudden shift in air. Clare was already staring tilt-headed at him. Why? Was he so different, or rather, was the difference so apparent? He marched forward, over the spot where he'd once frozen. Someone, still seated, shoved their chair backwards. It scraped across the floor and bumped a table. A folded scrap of paper pinned beneath a leg was knocked free. He didn't stop at the counter, Benjamin Tate – or was he Ben again, on the way to becoming Ben again? – instead, he went directly behind the counter to where she stood, watching him, mouth still agape. He put his two hands on her cheeks and pulled her towards him and kissed her. Not like that, not like that at all, more like a father might kiss his grown-up daughter.

'When do you finish?'

'Two.'

'I'll be back then.'

And then he was gone, the glass door swinging shut behind him, the café coming back to life. A hand reached down and placed the folded paper back beneath the table leg.

Benjamin Tate surged on. He wanted to run, not just to get to where he was going quicker, although he did, but to do something with this well of energy inside him. A new lease of life; that's what survivors said, wasn't it? That was him now, back from the dead, risen off the slab, stomping away as the man in the mask waved a scalpel after him. He looked up. In front of him the vast white building dominated the skyline, ever huge and hulking in the midst of the low suburbs. It appeared changed though, this morning, or maybe it was only his eyes that were changed. It didn't appear as the brute he'd always taken it for, rather a great, sad, cumbersome beast, self-conscious of its size. He felt a strange fondness for the old thing, wondered if he'd not misjudged it all these years, that actually it, too, had been forever out of place.

His black shoes echoed down the stairwell. He began calculating how many times he'd gone up and down them. Who cared? He opened the door and was surprised by how dim it was down there. Had it always been like this? He couldn't countenance it. Surely a bulb must have blown. Through the gloom he saw Pete and Sophia at their desks. As he got nearer they looked up. Pete tapped his wrist, where a watch would be if he'd worn one, and shook his head in mock reproof. Sophia smiled. He realised that she didn't like him, had never liked him, that her politeness was only for Pete.

He sat down at his desk, stared at the monitor, the keyboard, a notepad – he wondered idly what it was they thought he should have been writing in it all these years. Beside it was the batch of cards left over from the previous evening. Eastburn, Easter, Eastman... He opened the drawer and removed the bookmark, ran a light fingertip over the bulging letters, wondered how that man from the bench must have felt when he realised he'd lost it. This was the reason he'd gone back, he might never have returned otherwise, but how could he live with himself had he left it here to come apart, waste away, all alone in the dark. He put the bookmark in his pocket and stood up, reaching behind Sophia and extending his hand to Pete. Pete stared at it, uncomprehending. 'That's it for me,' Benjamin Tate said.

In years to come, when he remembered this day, and he would remember this day, he'd remember above all the sound of Pete hollering and whooping and clapping as he walked towards the door.

The mid-morning streets were empty. Everyone, it seemed, had things to do, places to be. He looked about. What struck him was the light. Perhaps it was just its contrast to the mute light downstairs, but it seemed unusually lucid that morning. He thought of the phrase, *liquid light*, thought this is what it probably meant. Everything seemed to radiate with a sort of translucence, a new clarity, their edges suddenly sharper than before. It made whatever he focused on stand out, almost jump out, from whatever was behind it. He thought how clear it was, how easy to see where one thing started and another ended.

He returned to his flat and searched the rooms for things to take with him. He looked in his cupboard, saw the shirts all lined up neatly with each flat sleeve holding the waist of the one in front, all in dull, vague shades of blue and brown and black, lifeless colours, colours that backgrounds were made of. He looked, a little guiltily, at the gown and slippers on the stool, imagined them peeking at him hopefully when he turned away. Did they know something was up, like a dog knows before its master goes on holiday? He walked out of the room, past the kitchen and into the lounge. The chair with its cross-eyed buttons, the single, small table, the shattered television. He had the sense as he moved about that this wasn't his home, that someone he'd never met had died here and he'd been sent to clear up. He glanced at the books; what time now, for other people's stories? As he walked out he fancied he could hear the walls, the lights, the softly fidgeting appliances whispering to each other after him. They'd never liked him either. Had the crooked number four fallen down then, that last time? It would have been fitting if it had.

At two o'clock he was outside the café. Clare emerged shortly afterwards and they walked a little without talking. She seemed for the first time to be nervous around him, or edgy. She stopped, waiting for him to speak.

'I'm not sure how to start,' he said. He began to tell her that he was going away, that he wasn't sure when or where, or for how long, and that she should come with him. As he was talking he was watching her recede from him. He wasn't surprised, found himself not minding even. He wondered at the seismic shifts that occur without our knowing, or without our acknowledging them, at least. He tried to identify what secret communications had already taken place that had foretold this.

'Why are you asking me?' she eventually said. He wondered that also. They had simply run their course. She was indeed Florence Nightingale, and he'd been diagnosed, treated, discharged. There was an awkward moment then, when both tried to think of something appropriate to say, before she'd taken his hand, squeezed it quickly, and then, just like that, let him go. In another week they'd be strangers.

Where would he go now, he wondered? He had no idea. Had that really been Madeline, in the car? He could find her, if he wanted, he didn't doubt that. There were ways and means.

Benjamin Tate was in an ancient courtyard that trapped the sun. He was standing on its edge, head tipped up at an angle, staring into the warm yellow glow behind his eyelids. Where was he? Somewhere in southern Europe, or North Africa, somewhere else, anyway. There were high, flat skies and deep-blue bays with white edges. He hadn't known the ocean could be that colour.

He'd been there more than a month, had only come for a week but discovered, to his surprise, that he was a secret sun-worshipper, he who had always considered himself to be a child of the winter. In the courtyard around him other people drifted to and fro, came and went, paid him no heed. He leant back and scratched his shoulder blades against the hot stone wall. It surprised him how smooth it was. He thought of the thousands, millions of arms that must have brushed up against it over the years, rubbed away, through sheer persistence, its rough edges. He smiled weakly to himself; there were lessons there.

He walked out of the courtyard, followed the pebbled alleys into which, still, the tracks of chariots were cut. He wondered what it must have been like, the day the earth exploded and spilled its scorching innards on top of everyone. Their corpses, set rigid in hardened cases of ash, were all about, in all manner of poses, and all ages. He wished he was nineteen again, or rather, that he was the age he was, but had lived his life differently since he was nineteen. Perhaps if someone had taken the time to tell him what Clare had told him. Yes, why had no one said those things to him? He thought of his mother, deranged and ranting in that dismal home. He thought of his father, hollowed out by grief, gone cold in the chair. And his brother. When he thought of Charlie, or Charles, he thought only of himself, of the gap that had opened not closed over the years.

An image of the old tree outside his window appeared. It would be there now, unchanged, as it had been yesterday, as it would be tomorrow. Of all things, he missed that tree the most, its remote steadfastness. What did it care if his dreamy face was gazing at it or not? He liked that about it. There was once a boy who had dumped a bin liner of clothes on a doorstep. He wondered what had become of him. He hadn't been destroyed. He saw him still, bent over in the false light. He could return to him.

The sun was directly overhead now, it beat down against the back of his neck. His water bottle sweated in his hand. Somewhere a boy was crying down at his dropped ice cream, watching it turn to pink liquid. Benjamin Tate found a bench, leaned down against his elbow and gazed dully at the shadow hunched between his feet. He closed his eyes again, thought he might drift away. All the voices swirling around him. A woman, old-sounding, was on her way to Oman to visit her husband, but had always wanted to visit this site. A man wasn't happy with his hotel bed, which creaked and kept him awake at night and he didn't sleep well at the best of times. So many lives. And what of his own now? Perhaps he'd run a marathon, or limp one at least, or set off on one of those hare-brained, cross-continental adventures that were all the rage these days, or he could climb a mountain, or all the mountains, or learn a new language. Perhaps he'd make a friend. No one is ever just one person.

Just behind him someone was speaking quietly, but he could hear every word she said, as though she were at his ear, talking only to him. She was speaking about a bench in a park, and a painting of an old ship on a wall, and a field of yellow rapeseed. She was saying she wanted to go back there. He heard another voice then, a young boy, no, two young boys, they sounded so alike, they were playing together. Soon their father would come and scoop them up with his two great paws and carry them home.

Benjamin Tate was on his feet now. It was cooler. The sun was off in a far corner of the sky. How long had he been there? Where had the time gone? He was running to catch up with it. The ruins were behind him. He heard another voice. He knew it, although he'd never heard it before. *I'm happy here*, it said. *And Mummy and Daddy will come soon.* Yes, he knew that voice. He would speak her name. Ruby. *Ruby.*

THE END

ALSO BY ALAN FELDBERG

Fall From Grace

ABOUT THE AUTHOR

Alan Feldberg is an author and journalist.

He writes literary fiction and psychological crime, with a keen focus on the human condition.

Previous works include Fall From Grace, and his many influences include John Banville, Richard Ford, Elizabeth Strout, Flannery O'Connor and Roddy Doyle.

Alan has travelled extensively and now lives in Yorkshire with his wife and daughters.

A NOTE FROM THE PUBLISHER

Thank you for reading this book. If you enjoyed it please do consider leaving a review on Amazon to help others find it too.

We hate typos. All of our books have been rigorously edited and proofread, but sometimes mistakes do slip through. If you have spotted a typo, please do let us know and we can get it amended within hours.

info@bloodhoundbooks.com

www.ingramcontent.com/pod-product-compliance
Lightning Source LLC
Chambersburg PA
CBHW061431210726
48287CB00007B/2171